FATED TO THE ALIEN GRUMP

WARRIORS OF TAVIKH

BOOK THREE

ERIN HALE

Fated to the Alien Grump
© 2024 by Erin Hale
Cover design by Natasha Snow

All Rights Reserved.

No part of this book, with the exception of brief quotations for book reviews or critical articles, may be reproduced or transmitted in any form or by any means, electronic or mechanical, including photocopying, recording, or by any information storage and retrieval system without express written permission from the author. This book may not be used in any way to train any AI.

This is a work of fiction. Names, characters, places, and incidents are the product of the author's imagination or are used fictitiously, and any resemblance to actual persons, living or dead, business establishments, events, or locales is entirely coincidental.

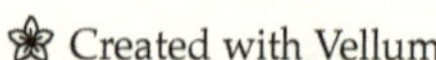 Created with Vellum

CONTENT WARNINGS
*MAY CONTAIN SPOILERS

As someone who doesn't have any triggers, it is often hard for me to know what might be a trigger for others. I have done my best to include what I think could potentially be triggering for someone. If I have not included yours, I apologize and hope you reach out so I know for the future.

Discussion of suicide
Discussion of previous off-page SA
Off-page DV
Off-page death of a child
Death of animals from hunting

CHAPTER I

If your book opens to this page, please refer to prior page for CW

Two months ago

Maeve

Sweat trickles down my back and nausea churns in my stomach. I take measured breaths, positive that everyone around me scurrying like a colony of ants can hear my heart pounding. A loud voice calls out to someone who replies back equally loudly, and I jump both times.

The area near the cargo hold of the Exodus Voyager is teeming with red uniform-wearing crew members loading supplies as well as the luggage of the passengers embarking on a two-month journey. I roll my shoulders and keep my chin tucked trying to make myself smaller.

Invisible.

A shadow stretches across the ground before a body crashes into me. I nearly cry out in pain and my fist clenches tightly around my suitcase handle. I bite my lip so hard the far-too familiar copper flavor fills my mouth.

"Watch where you're going," a rough voice complains.

I keep my head down and there's a moment of regret that I no longer have my long hair to hide behind. "Sorry." The apology is a reflexive whisper.

The man grunts and his footsteps fade away. I lift my gaze only long enough to gauge how close I am to the pile of luggage waiting to be loaded. Almost there. Reaching down, I make sure the name tag looped around the handle is still there. *Maeve Anderson.* That's who the suitcase belongs to. Or *belonged* to rather. Now it's mine.

Finally, the mountain of cotton sacks and suitcases similar to the one I carry appears in my line of sight and I add mine to it. With a final glance to make sure no one's paying attention to me, I make my way to the long winding ramp that will take me into the belly of the ship. The atmosphere is almost morose and no one has that jittery excited expression. Well, maybe a couple people do. But the number is so few they almost don't count.

Parents grip children's hands tightly as they funnel into the lined-up crowd at the base of the ramp that's my desti-nation. I slide in the narrow gap between what I assume is two separate families—one with a single child, the other with two—doing everything I can to make it appear as though I'm with one of them. While I suspect there are plenty of lone passengers boarding, the more I can blend in, the better.

Still, there's a niggling feeling of dread low in my stomach that I'm not going to make it onto the ship. I clench my fingers together at my waist to stop them from trembling. We're moving way too slow. If I can get inside, I can disappear. Hide out, until all the doors close and no one else is allowed to board.

"Are you excited?" a voice whispers next to me.

My head whips to the side and my heart jumps into my throat. One of the young girls, maybe eight or nine years old, stares up at me. Her long blonde hair falls in a braid on either side of her head and she's missing one of her bottom teeth.

I nod, clear my throat, and lie. "Yes. Are you?"

She glances at the two adults in front of her and leans in closer. "I'm scared. What if I don't like Tavikh? What if I don't make any friends?"

I'm not sure why she's asking me. Maybe I'm safer to talk to about her fears than her parents. I stare down at her and see myself. My old self. The young girl I was before my parents died and we'd all been happy. I don't want her to wind up like me, so I put on my best smile. Hopefully she can't tell it's forced and not even real.

"Think of it as an adventure. When you grow up and have kids, you'll get to tell them about this amazing trip you took on a spaceship across galaxies. You can tell them how much fun it was growing up on Tavikh where we get to have real houses and yards to play in. What's not to be excited about that?"

Slowly a twinkle enters her eyes and she bobs her head slightly. "You're right. I bet all the girls from our sector would be jealous if they knew what they were missing out on."

I'm not sure I'd go that far, but I agree with her anyway.

"Thank you. I'm Lucy," she introduces herself.

"Ka—" I cough. "Maeve."

Luckily, she doesn't notice my slip up. I check to see if anyone else might have. No one appears to be paying attention to us. Some of the tension leaves my shoulders and I unclench my fingers. Apparently, her mind eased about our journey, Lucy widens the gap between us and walks next to her mother. I take another step and my foot lands on the threshold of the ramp. This is it.

Keeping my head slightly facing toward the ship and away from the throng of people moving around the outer edges of the massive landing pad I make my way up. The journey is painstakingly slow. I keep waiting for someone to call out my name and drag me off the ramp.

The darkened interior of the ship grows closer and larger until, at last, I'm inside. It's not as dark as it appears from the outside. Recessed lights in the ceiling cast a warm glow over the metal walls and floor. We travel down hallway after hallway making so many turns that there's no way I could find my way back to the entrance. After another turn, the passageway opens into a large, high-ceiling room with rows of seats that stretch from one side of it to the other. There's a narrow aisle breaking each row in half.

I continue following Lucy and her family until they find a group of seats together. Yanking my crumpled ticket from my pocket, I read over it and search for a seat number or anything to designate where I should go. The only thing it says is general seating. I'm going to take that to mean we can sit wherever we want. I search for an empty spot. Preferably in the back and away from others.

Finally, I settle into a seat that faces the entrance. I don't want to be caught unaware if someone shows up looking for me. Maybe hours or only minutes go by, but the number of people trickling in slows. I don't make eye contact with anyone. Instead, I keep my head down, my hands in my lap, and pray we take off soon.

At long last the ship rumbles, and the seat beneath me vibrates. The vibration triggers pain that reverberates through my cracked ribs, and I clench my teeth hard enough I worry I might break them. There's only the slightest downward pressure, and then it levels out. The room is windowless, so I can't even look outside to confirm we left the ground.

Ten, maybe fifteen, minutes pass, and the ship shakes and rattles again, significantly more than it had before. I close my eyes and take deep breaths through the pain—willing myself not to get sick everywhere—until the motion smooths out. Seconds pass and static crackles from the speakers overhead.

"This is Captain Blanchard speaking. We have exited Earth's atmosphere and begun our flight to the planet Tavikh. Staterooms and the dining hall are located on the second level. You will find a fitness room and passenger rec room on the main level. Crew members will be circulating through the ship if you have any questions. Otherwise, enjoy the trip."

I wait for more, but the voice that had come from the ceiling remains silent. Blessedly, the pain lessens and I breathe easier. Several people release their safety harnesses and head out of the cabin, I guess to explore the massive ship that's our home for the next two months.

Trying not be obvious, I take in the other passengers. No one looks familiar. Of course, New St. Louis is the home of over two million people, and more than half of them live in the bottom tier like me. The chances of someone I know being here are slim. It's one of the reasons this was my escape plan. Well, more like Chelsea's escape plan. She's the only person left on Earth that I trust.

I remain seated until my rear goes numb, and I'm almost the only one left within the passenger cabin. I take out my ticket again where I'd been told my room number would be located. All I want to do is go hide there. I need to find out if there are scheduled meals or if we're free to go to the cafeteria whenever we're hungry. If that's that case, I'll plan my visits for when there should be the least amount of people.

After unlatching my safety harness, I slowly rise. I'm stiff and achy from sitting so long, and there's a throbbing pain in my ribs. A bruise covers my entire side, and if history is any indication, it will be there for a while.

I make my way down a hallway, reading each placard I pass to guide me in the right direction. After only getting turned around once, I come to a stop in front of room fifteen-oh-one. I pause before placing my hand on the bioscanner. I'd freaked out when Chelsea took me to pick up my ticket for the trip, but she assured me everything would be okay.

When we stepped up to the counter, and I laid my clammy hand on the cold glass so it could scan my palm, the woman seated behind it glanced first at my friend and then at me. I still can't be certain, but I could almost swear Chelsea gave a nod so slight no one would notice.

"Maeve Anderson," the woman said. "One-way ticket to Tavikh. Here you go."

She stamped the paper and passed it over to me. With trembling fingers, I took it and quickly stashed it in my pocket before she realized she'd made a mistake. That had been a week ago. Every day since, I worried someone would come pounding on my door, but they never did. Taking a deep breath, I lay my palm on the bioscanner, and the door opens with a whoosh.

A glaringly bright light automatically turns on inside the room, and I freeze at the sight of a woman lying in the bottom bunk.

"I'm sorry, I didn't realize anyone was in here already." I didn't realize anyone was in here at all.

She sits up and pushes her hair back off her face. "It's okay. Hi, um, I'm London. I guess we must be roommates."

I'll look like an idiot if I just keep standing here staring, so I step inside and wrap my arms around myself, not quite meeting her eye. *Remember your name.* "Maeve." Having to be in the same room as someone means always keeping my guard up. How am I going to do this for two months?

"It's nice to meet you. My bag was already on this bed, but if you'd rather have it, I'll take the top one."

I shake my head. "No, it's fine."

Other than Chelsea, I don't make friends. They always wind up dying, or I get screwed over in some way.

An uncomfortable silence settles between us.

"Um, would you like to unpack your things? You have first dibs on which side of the dresser you want. I haven't put anything in there yet," London says.

Silently, I pad across the room, and without looking at her, pull my suitcase off the top bunk, set it on the dresser, and put away every possession I own. It doesn't take more than a minute. I close my now empty suitcase, not sure where to store it. The room is small with no closet.

"You can slide your empty luggage under the bunk if you want. I promise I won't bother it." London stands and moves a few steps away.

Briefly I hesitate before I take it over, carefully squat, and slide it under her bed. "Thanks."

"No problem. So, is this your first time in space? It is mine, and I thought I was going to barf before we even made it through the outer atmosphere," she babbles without pausing between sentences, and for the first time I relax.

I guess London's just as nervous as me. The thought makes me feel better, and I manage a small smile. "Me too. I hadn't expected so much shaking."

"Oh my god, it was the worst. I'm glad it didn't last long. I would have embarrassed myself," she admits. "You can have a seat if you want."

"Thanks."

We both head to the small table at the same time, and London's sudden movement makes me jump away instinctively. She freezes and gives me a strange look. My cheeks heat and I stride over to the chair, trying to act as nothing weird just happened. She finally moves and sits across from me. Another short, awkward moment, but I scold myself for treating her this way. She's perfectly nice. I relax slightly and try to make up for my shortness with conversation.

"Have you been anywhere else on the ship yet?" I'm pretty sure she'd been sleeping when I walked in.

"My friend Remi and I did a little exploring shortly after takeoff," London says. "We scouted out what they called the training room. I'm not really athletic, so I don't think I'll get much use out of it, but Remi seemed excited about being in there. Afterward, we ate in the cafeteria. I must have fallen asleep when I got back here, so I'm not sure how long ago that was. Oh, and we met another woman about our age. Zara. Her room is actually next door, and Remi is on the other side of her."

"Did you and Remi come together?" I ask.

She shakes her head with a little laugh. "Oh, no, she sort of adopted me, I guess. We were sitting across from each other during takeoff. Pretty sure she was afraid I was going to throw up all over her."

I chuckle because there'd been a moment where I thought I'd do the same thing. "I'm sure she's glad you didn't."

"No more than I am." She pauses and I stiffen, a sense of dread settling in my gut. "I take it you're going to Tavikh for a…change of scenery like the rest of us?"

Fear that she'll find out my secret makes my vision go dark, but I quickly blink it away and try to smooth out my expression. "Something like that."

"I promise I won't pry," London rushes to assure me. "Whatever reasons you have are your own."

I nod shallowly and slightly roll my shoulders forward like I do when I try to stay invisible, but don't say anything else.

She clears her throat. "If you want, I can show you around the ship. Maybe we can find the passenger rec room the captain mentioned. Remi and I missed it during our search."

For several seconds, I weigh my response. I'm going to spend two months with this woman. I don't want things being weird between us the entire time. I want to be able to relax. Maybe even let my guard down for once. Maybe make a friend. "That would be nice."

"Great," London says and gets up.

I let her lead us out of the room, and in that moment, I decide to stop being afraid. Maybe this time, it'll stick.

CHAPTER 2

PRESENT DAY

Maeve

It didn't stick.

Not really. I've tried not being afraid, but every day we've been on Tavikh has been one more day with something to fear. The day we landed, a horde of aliens called Krijese attacked everyone getting off the ship. They are horrible and ugly with black snake-like ropey hair, vertically split mouths with fangs that open to expose razor-sharp teeth, and evil beady eyes. By the time the Tavikhi warriors arrived to rescue us, people had already died. *Lucy* died. I laid in my tent that night and cried myself to sleep.

London, Zara, Remi, our new friend Sage, and I lived through a second attack the next night only to now find ourselves living in the Tavikhi village, because London is somehow the fated mate of their leader. It's a place filled with massive lavender warriors with long, yellow-white hair who train for battle daily and walk around with swords hanging from belts at their waists.

It doesn't matter that we're only at the fire for the midday meal. I do everything I can to avoid people noticing me. Even if that means sitting on the ground—hiding—tucked in between my friends' legs. Because if I don't, one of these warriors might accidentally touch me and trigger their mating marks to appear like Zander's did with London. And nothing scares me as much as the Tavikhi men do.

"Do you guys want to go back to the tent for a little while and play Pebbles?" Zara asks as soon as we finish eating.

Sage shakes her head. "Sorry, I need to head to the medicine tent. One of the warriors injured during the attack on the settlement needs his wound checked and re-bandaged. Plus, I'm working on making a new cream formula for us humans. I don't know about you, but my skin gets chapped in the winter, and there's not much here in the way of skin protection. So, I'm making some. Or at least trying to."

"Yeah, and I need to meet Rassim soon for our next training session," Remi tells her.

Zara glances down at me and I wince, because I know how much she's struggling to find something around the village to do that she's good at. "I told Alanda I would help her harvest some of the roots and spices after the midday meal."

"Maybe this is the perfect opportunity for you to approach Benham about becoming an apprentice," Sage suggests to Zara with a tip of her chin. "He at least looks like he's in a reasonable mood."

We all swivel to stare at the warrior in question. I shudder. He's the biggest Tavikhi in the entire village. The sixteen or so humans who decided to come here after the second Krijese attack avoid him like the plague. He's covered in scars, including one that runs down the entire right side of his face from his hairline to his chin.

Even terrified, I can admit the Tavikhi males are attractive and the females beautiful. Benham's scar doesn't make him any less attractive. It just makes him appear harder. I still can't believe Zara's considering asking him if she can apprentice for him with his weapon making.

Next thing we know, she takes a deep breath, stands, and makes her way over to where he towers over another warrior. She comes to a stop just short of them and the male in question turns to face her while the other one walks away. If Benham glared down at me the way he is her, I'd probably pee myself. With arms crossed and the ever-present scowl on his face, he gives the appearance that he hates not just humans, but the world. A flare of panic flutters in my chest.

"Does anyone want to take a bet that he's going to make her cry?" Sage stage whispers.

London, Remi, and I spent two months on a ship with Zara. Sage doesn't know her well enough yet. Remi shakes her head. "Zara is made of much sterner stuff than that.

She's pretty fearless. Sometimes to an extreme. I wouldn't bet against her."

"What are you all staring at?" London ask as she takes Zara's spot on the bench and twists partway toward where our gazes are all focused.

"Zara's talking to Benham about teaching her how to make weapons," Remi fills her in.

She whips fully around to stare. I'm stunned he hasn't sent Zara away. Instead, he's actually talking to her. Or maybe he's chastising her for some offense like daring to speak to him. It's hard to tell with the never-shifting glower. Before long, he nods and walks away. I count the seconds until she finally turns around. There's a stunned expression on Zara's face. Not fear. But utter shock.

She rushes over. "Oh my god, he said yes."

He did? Why? Being so focused on my surroundings makes it easy to notice everything going on around me. I pay close attention to everyone in the village. And Benham's made it more than obvious exactly what he thinks about us humans. London and Zara playfully bicker about him and his attitude.

"He wants me to meet him at his forge."

"Now?" Remi gapes.

"He said I might as well get started." Zara nods. "Of course, as he was leaving, I heard him grumble something under his breath about humans. But I'm not going to let his sourness ruin anything. He's probably trying to see if I can handle his cranky ass. Benham doesn't know who he's dealing with yet."

I reach out for her hand and squeeze it in encouragement. Just because I don't understand why she's so excited about learning from Benham, doesn't mean I can't be happy for her and wish her well. "I have faith in you."

"Aw, thanks Mae."

Rassim, our friend Alanda's mate, approaches the group and greets London first and us after. He and Remi trade barbs before they split off and head for their training session. The rest of us say our goodbyes and I go in search of Alanda, doing my best to avoid eye contact with anyone. It takes everything I have to walk through the village alone and not spend all my time hiding in my tent. My gaze constantly sweeps the area around me, making sure I know where everything and every*one* is. I may be hyper-vigilant and a tad paranoid, but I don't care.

I make it to Alanda's tent and tap on the hide flap that serves as a door. Seconds later, she sweeps it open.

"Greetings, Maeve."

"Hi."

"Have you finished with your meal?"

I nod. "Yeah, so I'm ready whenever you are."

Alanda exits the tent with her long hair intricately braided and leads me to the garden where all the herbs used for cooking are grown. I glance over at her and can't help but compare us. She wears the typical outfit of most of the female Tavikhi: a bandeau type top and a long flowing skirt that nearly brushes the ground and exposes her bare feet with each step she takes. It's a weird simple elegance. A vast difference from the jeans, tennis shoes, and baggy Henley I'm wearing. These aren't even my clothes. They're ones Chelsea packed for me for my trip here.

We stop at the large garden and its rows of different herbs I still haven't learned all the names of yet. I'm working on it, though. Even though the product is a far cry from what I made at the factory back on Earth, it's similar in its monotony of harvesting stack after stack of the same thing. There's a familiarity to it that makes me feel comfortable.

"I will let you start with the rashem. If it has turned a darker color at the base, then it is ready to be picked." Alanda points to the section of the garden where she wants me to go.

Together, we work to gather small bundles of the bitter smelling herb. It smells like the leburin stew we frequently eat. I came across the tanning tent once and walked in on a few of the females and an elder skinning what could only be described as an alien rabbit without the poofy tail or long ears. I try not to think about what I'm eating, since I know what it looks like before. Maybe that's a benefit of living in the bottom tier with a primary diet of protein bars. There's no worry I'm eating a cute little animal.

After three rows, I have a nice stack of rashem built up. I set them in a small pile off to one side of the garden and move to the row of root vegetables. Alanda is a few rows away. Sometimes I miss working with Mary. She was a gossip, but it was nice to hear the sound of someone's voice. And she was nothing if not entertaining. The near quiet isn't too bad though, I suppose, if one can ignore the sounds of warriors sparring down in the training arena. Just different. Like everything else on this planet.

I pause to arch my back and lift my gaze to the sky. If the aliens weren't proof I was on an alien planet, the purple sky would certainly give it away. It's not even the purple that comes with a pretty sunrise or sunset. It's a bright lavender color maybe a shade darker than the Tavikhi people. Once the sun sets on this long day, two moons will fill the sky. It's hard to imagine this is my life.

"Is all well, Maeve?" Alanda asks.

I turn my head her way. "Yeah, I'm just stretching and thinking about how different the sky is here than back on Earth."

"Do you miss your home?"

There are aspects I miss like the familiarity of everything and, of course, Chelsea. Otherwise, I'm glad to see the last of it. "No, not really." Earth wasn't too kind to me.

"We are glad you and your tribe sisters are here," Alanda says.

Yeah, they're glad because London just happens to be the mate of their leader and maybe their numbers will start growing if the two of them manage to have babies. Shame burns inside me at the uncharitable thought. When did I become so bitter? "Thank you. We're glad to be here as well."

She folds her hands in front of her and darts a quick glance away in a shy manner she doesn't usually present to me. Only London. "I, especially, am glad you are here. There are only a few females of a similar age to me, and none have met their mate yet. After I awakened Rassim's mating marks, my other tribe sisters slowly withdrew themselves from me. I am thankful for the friendship you, the shefira, and the other human females have shown me."

 Damn it. Now I feel extra shitty for my cynical thoughts. Although, what she says doesn't surprise me. I guess Tavikhi women aren't all that different from Earth women in that regard. "I'm sorry that has happened to you. I guess it's a good thing then, that the humans don't have such a concept as mates. So there's no reason for us to be envious of your relationship with Rassim."

Alanda's bony brow ridges dip. "Humans do not mate?"

"Not in the way Tavikhi do. There's no such thing as fate or mating marks."

"Then how do you know who your mate is?"

How to explain this. "If you see someone you're attracted to, you can ask them out on a date. Like to hang out and do stuff with. Sometimes one date turns into a bunch of dates and two people eventually fall in love and get married—mated. But other times, you go out on one date and realize you don't want to go out on another date with them, so you go looking for a different person to ask out."

"What if you pick the wrong person to be your mate?" Alanda cocks her head.

"I suppose you get divorced and keep searching."

"Divorced?"

"Um, like you break the marriage bond."

Her feline eyes widen. "Humans can break a mating bond? Do neither of them go on to the lands of your goddess?"

I gape. "You mean, like, die? Is that what happens to Tavikhi? If the bond is broken one of them dies?" What the hell?

Alanda shakes her hand and I breath a sigh of relief. "A mating bond is never broken. Not even in death. If either the male or female dies, then their mate follows them on their journey to the lands of Deeka."

What? Holy hell. Surely that wouldn't happen with London and Zander. Would it? Does she know about this?

Just one more reason to not want one of the men touching me. We go back to picking the rest of our hoard for the day, but I'm even more subdued than usual.

That night at the evening meal, I can't help but study the mated pairs that linger around the central fire. I've never been particularly religious, but I say a small prayer to anyone who might be listening that none of the Tavikhi warriors are my mate.

CHAPTER 3

BENHAM

I douse the flames of the forge for the night and carefully stow my supplies. My new apprentice—one I never expected to have, and especially not a human female—has already left to meet her tribe sisters at the central fire. Zara boldly approached me several mornings ago and said she wanted to learn weapon making. I stared down at her like I have many of the young warriors I train to fight to determine if she will continue meeting my gaze head on or glance away. To my surprise she kept eye contact with me. To my greater surprise, I agreed to teach her.

After I double-check no embers remain, I make my way to my tent to wash off the dust that clings to my skin. Someone has come in to tend the fire and the welcoming warmth greets me. I strip off my leg coverings and take the cloth from the table, dip it in the water basin, and clean myself. Drawing a fresh pair from my storage chest, I dress and head for the central fire.

On my approach, there is a commotion at the front gate. I tense, having not brought a weapon with me, but exclamations of joy trickle through the tribespeople until it reaches those gathered for the evening meal. My gaze is drawn to Zander, our shefir. He stiffens and jumps to his feet, his gaze focused in the direction of the entrance to the village. Behind him his tail thrashes. There is only a brief hesitation before he strides forward.

He barely makes it to the other side of the central gathering place before he comes to an abrupt halt. I move to stand close by and I too stop at the sight coming toward us. Zydon, Zander's twin—as the humans call him—and his mate Remi, have returned from their trip along the outer border of our territory. But they are not alone.

Walking with an unfamiliar human female is Zedam, Zander and Zydon's younger brother, who has been missing and thought dead for many lunar cycles. Even in the dying light, his dark mating marks are obvious. An air of excitement, relief, and hope fill the air.

Our tribe brother is home.

The shefira comes to Zander's side and places her hand in his. Finally, Zedam and his mate—surrounded by all our tribespeople—come to a stop in front of our shefir. They stare at each for several moments until they both move at once and embrace. Zander says something to his brother, but it is too low for me to hear. They draw back and rest their brow bones against the other's.

"My brother, we have missed you so," Zander rasps out.

"And I you," Zedam says. "I have much to tell you, but there is someone I want you to meet."

The two separate, and the small female steps forward. Zedam's tail wraps around her waist and his arm goes around her shoulder to bring her tightly against his side.

"This is Eloise," he says, pride evident in his tone. "My *keeshla*."

"It's nice to meet you," the female says and sticks her hand out like I have seen the humans do when greeting someone.

Zander takes it in both of his and presses his brow bone to the top of it. "Thank you for bringing my brother home. I am happy to call you sister."

He releases her and draws London to him. "And this is my mate, London."

"Welcome home," our shefira says.

Zedam's gaze shifts and meets mine. His lips curl in a smile, and he separates from his mate and closes the distance between us. "Benham."

I grip his forearm and fist my chest. He does the same.

"We are glad to see you alive."

"Thank you, brother. None more so than I."

"Come, let us all sit around the fire and eat and Zedam can tell us his tale," Zander calls out. "Afterward we will celebrate the return of our tribe brother and welcome our new tribe sister."

Excited yells fill the air as everyone cheers. Many tribespeople approach Zedam and his mate, welcoming his return. Eventually, we all settle to eat. Afterward, Zedam tells us of the battle he fought against two Krijese all those lunar cycles ago. Wounded, he stumbled into the forest, and collapsed. When he awoke, there were nothing but blank spaces filling his head. He did not know who he was or where he came from. He traveled alone for many turns of the sun, but never found another village. So he settled within a small clearing and made his home there until his *keeshla* fell from the sky in an escape pod twenty turns of the sun ago. It took several more turns, another Krijese attack, and another a blow to his head, for all the blank spaces inside it to fill back up.

"We have traveled for twelve turns of the sun to reach the village, but we have finally returned home." Zedam ends his tale.

"Much has changed since you have been gone," Zander tells him. "Many Krijese from King Armik's village fled and have made their new home within the hills. They have spoken to Zydon and want nothing more than peace, as they are dying out. The king and his remaining warriors attacked us four turns of the sun ago. He no longer lives, nor do most of his warriors. For now, we hope that means they will cease trying to make war on us or the human settlement."

With the threat of the Krijese gone, perhaps the humans will return to their village. I am not sure why they came in the first place when up until perhaps two turns of the sun ago they have stayed to themselves and keep their kits away from ours. More than once, I have snapped harsh words at their cowardly males.

The shefira is working hard to help bridge the gap between the humans and the Tavikhi, but I doubt she will be successful. They do almost nothing and rely on us to provide for them without contributing in any way. I want to tell her not to bother, but it is not my place.

As the tribespeople prepare for the celebration, I head for my tent at the far end of the village. Despite the distance, noise will travel, so it is going to be a long night. Inside, I sit on the low seat my baba's baba crafted many seasons ago. It is one of the few remaining things I have of my ancestors. Drawing out one of my many swords and a stone, I work on sharpening the edges.

As the sounds of the celebration around the fire reach me, I continue with my work. While I am happy for the return of Zedam, who we all thought long-dead, I have no desire to be around all the tribespeople or the noise. I prefer my solitude.

It is cowardly to hide in here.

I curse the voice inside my head. It is not cowardice nor is it hiding. I have never been one for people. Even as a kit. Having Zander, Zydon, and Zedam as my closest friends—brothers—has been enough. Besides, there is no sense in befriending anyone when they could die in the next Krijese attack. The same way my baba and nene had. Slaughtered by our enemies while patrolling together outside the village. It is best to keep people at a distance.

Another bout of laughter filters through the hide of my dwelling. It is feminine and not Tavikhi. Considering the few humans who moved into our village spend most of their time avoiding us, it must be one of the shefira's tribe sisters. The tribespeople are still in disbelief that the last spaceship from Terra to land on Tavikh contained Zander's fated mate. And now, it would seem, Zydon's as well.

Every unmated warrior in the village—who had previously resigned themselves to the fact they would never find a mate—has done nothing but talk about these humans. Our shefir has offered them protection from the moment the first ship landed many lunar cycles ago despite the fact they are weak, lazy, and selfish. Even the ones who now reside here. The only exceptions I have found are the shefira and her closest tribe sisters, although I do not know them well.

A small bout of guilt creeps in that I am sitting in my tent when I could be doing something more useful than sharpening swords that are already sharp. I make my way to the healer's tent. Several of our warriors were injured in the recent Krijese attack. I step inside and prop my staff against the hide just inside the door. All three raised platforms are occupied by the warriors with the most grievous injuries while several makeshift pallets have been placed on the ground for the lesser injured.

Kyler glances up from where he is changing a bandage on one of our fallen brothers. "Benham, is all well?"

"Aye. I merely came to check on the wounded and see if you needed anything."

If the healer is surprised at my offer, he hides it. He glances at his human apprentice. "Sage, is there anything you need?"

The female, who is cleaning someone's wound, gestures to the table nearest her. "I could use some fresh, warm water. Our supply is low, and I don't have time to head to the river myself."

She should not be going there in the dark anyway. The humans do not see as well as we do, and it may not be safe. I nod at Kyler. "I will return."

Grabbing the large vessel that is nearly empty, I take it to the river and fill it. Once I return to the healer's tent, I place it over the fire to heat.

"Thank you," the female says, glancing up briefly before returning to her task.

Since neither of them ask for help with anything else, it would appear there is nothing left for me to do. I quickly check on each warrior. All are being well taken care of. I exit the tent, not as focused as I should be. I've barely made it two steps when a tiny, soft body collides with mine. Instinctively, I drop my weapon and catch the female before she falls. My hands burn, and I growl at the brief burst of pain that slowly subsides into a warm tingling sensation that travels up my arms and across my sides.

I stare down into the face of one of the shefira's closest tribe sisters. The small, quiet one. Her eyes, the color of which I have never seen before, widen in alarm and she shakes her head. Only a few heartbeats pass, and her denial is coming in words that grow louder with each one as she pushes herself away, hard, from my chest.

"No. No, no, no."

I release her just as quickly as I caught her and take a step away to give her room. I do my best to ignore the darkening glow of the mating marks on my arms. The healer's assistant rushes out of the tent.

"What's going on? Oh, shit," Sage curses and moves between the tiny female and me, so I lose sight of her. "It's okay, Maeve."

Maeve. The female's name—my *mate's* name—is Maeve.

"Hey, you're all right. Why don't we head to the tent and get out of this cold? You're shivering." Sage picks the fur up off the ground and the tiny female's gaze locks onto mine again. There is so much fear in her eyes, like the dreri who scents a predator on the air.

Sage wraps the fur around Maeve, guides her away from me, and glances over her shoulder. "Benham, you should probably go get London, Zara, and Remi."

The instruction wakes me from my state. I grab my staff from the ground and head to the central fire, where the celebration is still going strong. After a few steps, I hesitate but then shake my head. My mating marks will be obvious to everyone whether it is tonight or in the morning. There is no hiding them.

I continue walking. It is Jodah who spots me first. His eyes widen just as Maeve's did, but in his, there is envy. I ignore his stare and head for the shefira. Zara turns toward me.

"Oh, fuck."

At her curse, everyone's attention is on me. The thing I hate the most. More eyes widen and they all stare in stunned silence. She, Remi, and the shefira break away and rush over, all of them on unsteady feet. No doubt from the special brew the elders bring out for celebrations.

"Sage would like to see you in her tent."

My apprentice's shoulders relax, and she breathes out a sigh. "So Sage is your mate, huh? I didn't she—*see*—that one coming. Is she okay?"

"No."

"No, she's not okay?" Remi asks.

"She is not my mate."

"Oh, fuck," Zara repeats.

CHAPTER 4

My whole body is numb and cold, even with the fire blazing. All I can do is sit and stare into it and keep asking myself what bad things I've done that I deserve this punishment. I've always tried to be a good person. I would often work through my ten minute break so my co-worker Mary could go outside and hang out with her boyfriend while he was on his break. We had a daily quota to fill so I would stack extra cover plates so she'd reach hers.

I can sense Sage's presence, but she hasn't said anything more since she brought me in here. Or if she has, I haven't heard it over the swishing sound in my ears. The flames in front of me dance and sway, and dark shadows fill the tent. Muffled sounds come from far away and slowly penetrate. There's a light touch against my arm and I flinch.

"Maeve," a voice whispers. "It's me, London. Zara, Remi, and Sage are here too."

Great. Apparently everyone gets to witness my mental breakdown. Beside me the furs move and someone sits close, but not touching. Same with the other side. Two bodies move in front of me blocking my view of the fire.

I blink, and London's face comes into focus.

She reaches for me and hesitates. "I'm going to hold your hands, okay?"

I guess she takes my silence as permission, because her fingers close around mine. Warmth seeps into them. No one else speaks. We all sit there in the quiet. The only sound disturbing the air is the occasionally pop of the fire. I have no idea how much time passes before London speaks again.

"You don't have to—and none of us will pressure you to—but will you tell us what happened?"

Do they mean before? Or tonight? Although I suppose one leads into the other. I'm not sure how I thought none of my secrets would ever come out. Then again, there's no reason they should have. I could have just kept going with this new life. But no. Some higher power thought differently.

"My name isn't Maeve Anderson," the words spill out in a gravelly whisper. "It's Katherine Waters. I'm from the factory sector. My friend Chelsea arranged for a new identity and a ticket on the Exodus Voyager."

I pause, still not ready to finish my story. London squeezes my hands. "You don't have to tell us anything else if you don't want to."

A rough laugh breaks through my throat. "I've told you this much. I might as well tell you the rest of it."

This is the most I've spoken in over two months. I have to clear the scratchiness from my throat. "A year ago, the son of the factory CEO where I work—worked—caught me outside. Said he'd seen me one day when touring the facility with his father. For the next month, he flirted with me. Brought me small gifts. Made me think I was special. I suppose you can figure out what happens after that."

"He seduced you." Remi doesn't phrase it as a question, but I nod anyway.

"I'd been alone for so long, and he paid special attention to me. I soaked every bit of it up." I laugh, but it's tinged with self-deprecation. "It took me a while to figure out I was only a novelty for him. Someone from the upper tier slumming it with someone from the bottom tier. He got possessive. If I tried going anywhere besides work, he wouldn't let me. If I even mentioned someone else's name, no matter who it was, he'd get angry. We fought all the time. I tried to break up with him, but he wouldn't leave me alone."

I have to take a breather to get through the rest. "At first, he just yelled and screamed at me. The first time he hit me, I threatened to go to the guards, and he laughed. Said no one would believe a bottomer like me. After he'd punched me a few too many times, his father found out through the whisper network at the factory. I believe *his* exact words were 'if you need to keep her in line, make sure it's not where people can see.'"

"What a cunt," Zara, who sits beside London, spits out. She glances around at our wide-eyed stares. "Don't look at me like that. You all were thinking the exact same thing."

"Thanks, Zar." I let go of one of London's hand and squeeze hers.

"What made you decide to come to Tavikh?" Remi asks.

"Because my only other option was to stay on Earth and die. A week before we got my ticket, David showed up at my room. I told him to leave, but he didn't listen. He pushed me inside, slammed the door closed, and then he —" I snap my mouth shut, not wanting to say any more, and I won't meet anyone's eyes. I had no desire to relive that night. "Anyway, he finally left. When I was able to drag myself out of bed, I commed Chelsea. She came over, got me cleaned up, and hid me in the upper tier where no one would think to look for me until I could get on the ship. And now…here I am."

None of my friends speak and the silence lengthens. Finally, I look at London. Tears stream down her face. Zara's too. In fact, they're all crying except me. I'm not sure when the last time I had. Crying didn't solve anything. London's the first to move. Slowly, she gets to her knees and ever so gently gives me a hug. Another weight is added to that as more arms twine around me, until I'm surrounded by the people I love.

Minutes later, they release me and sit back. Remi strokes my hair. "It's no wonder you don't want to be mated to Benham."

I don't want to be mated to *anyone*.

"As someone who has spent the most time around the Tavikhi," Sage speaks up. "I can tell you that Benham would never—none of them would—hurt you. I'm not saying you have to agree to the mating. I just thought it might ease your mind a little that, no matter what your decision is, you're safe."

I almost laugh. While I appreciate what she's trying to say, we haven't been safe since we landed on this planet.

"Nobody has to make any decisions tonight," London says with the confidence she's gaining in her position within the village of Shefira. "Everyone can try to get a good night's sleep and things will look bet—different in the morning."

At least she's not trying to pretend that everything is going to be better. Someone smacks the door flap.

"London? Is all well inside?"

I'm surprised Zander waited this long to check on his mate. He's rarely without her by his side. We joke they're attached at the hip, but it isn't far off. It gives me chills, even though I've never seen him raise his voice to her. She scrambles to her feet and pushes the flap open only enough to stick her head out. Their low tones reach me, but I can't make out what they're saying.

Zara reaches for my hands. "I'm not always an optimist, but everything's going to be okay. One way or another. All right?"

I nod, although I don't really believe it. London closes the hide door and returns to her place in front of me. "What do you guys think about a slumber party? The five of us staying up late—six if Eloise wants to join—talking about whatever we want to talk about? I'd say we could eat a bunch of junk food, too, but even on Earth we didn't have that. Well, some of us didn't. No offense Remi or Zara."

"None taken," Zara says with a half shrug. "I wasn't allowed to have junk food. Everything I ate was carefully chosen to keep me at the optimal weight."

Based on her use of air quotes with the last two words, I'm going to guess someone else said that to her. From hints she's dropped, it was probably her parents. I glance around at my friends. Other than Sage, whose story no one knows, we all had pretty shitty lives back on Earth. I doubt a slumber party will make me feel better, but there's a hopeful gleam in London's eyes I don't want to dash. She's doing her best to cheer me up.

"A sleepover might be fun," I try to sound enthusiastic.

"Excellent." She claps her hands. "I'll grab some extra furs from my tent and see if I can have Zander send someone out to bring us back some not-a-peaches."

Remi moans. "Oh my god, yes, please."

London laughs and gets up to leave, but I snag her hand. I stare up at her and at the others. "I'm really glad you guys are my friends."

"Are you kidding?" Remi says. "We're the lucky ones. No one can ask for a better friend than Maeve Anderson."

One side of my mouth curls. "You know that's not really my name, right?"

"It is to us," Zara says with a careless shrug. "You may have been Katherine Waters before you stepped onto that ship, but the minute you crossed the threshold, you became Maeve. We don't know who you used to be, and it doesn't matter. We know who you are now, and you're the sweetest, kindest, bravest, never-has-a-bad-thing-to-say-to anyone best friend any of us could ever have."

Okay so maybe a good cry on occasion isn't bad. Tears fill my eyes, but I swipe them away.

"I'll be back in a few minutes," London says. "Don't start having fun without me."

"We wouldn't dream of it," Remi replies with a bit too much playful sarcasm.

London narrows her eyes, and Remi gives her a not-so-innocent look. London shakes her head with a smile and walks out of the tent. Zara rifles around on her side of the tent and brings out the little case of stones we use to play Pebbles. We all groan good-naturedly, because if we've learned one thing over the last two months is that she makes up new rules of the game as she goes.

Maybe this sleepover will do me good. Something to take my mind off the Tavikhi warrior who scares the hell out of me.

CHAPTER 5

After the females leave, Zydon approaches with a large grin and grips my forearm. I can not help but compare my marks to his. While similar, they also differ both in design and location. They are also nothing I ever expected to have.

"This is wonderful news. Deeka continues to bless us," he says. "I am happy for you brother."

More tribespeople offer their good tidings, while I would like nothing more than to retreat to my tent. I do not let my irritation win. A newly mated pairing is a joyous occasion for our people, especially after having gone so many seasons without any until now. It represents a future for our tribe. Once the people return to their celebration, Zander comes to my side. Of the three brothers, I am closest with him.

"Let us sit." He moves to the place where he takes his meals and settles onto the flat surface.

I lower myself next to him and wait for him to speak. I have nothing to say, and why waste unnecessary words? It is what my baba taught me.

"It is Maeve who triggered your mating marks?"

"Yes."

"I do not know all of the humans' reasons for coming to Tavikh, but what I have learned from my *keeshla* is that life on their planet is often difficult," Zanders explains. "They come from a place that is divided into those with much wealth and those with none and the two do not co-exist. There is no common village where everyone helps those in need. It is often why they choose to leave. They believe they may have a better life on this planet."

A moment of silence passes before he claps me on the shoulder and rises.

"I know most of the unmated males have given up on ever finding their mate, even the younger ones like Rojtar. But we, you included, have now shown them that there *is* hope. Hope that one of these turns of the sun, they too will find their *keeshla* as we have. You have been blessed with yours for a reason."

Zander returns to the fire and the celebration that shows no signs of slowing down. I sit there for many beats of my heart staring into the flames until it is time for me to return to my tent. The fire still burns well, but I add one more piece of wood, and climb beneath my furs. My nene and baba were mated for thirty-three warm seasons before their death. As much as it pains me to admit, I am glad they went to the lands of Deeka together. I did not have to watch one of them waste away to nothing until they passed as well. That is how strong the bond is. If one mate dies, the other mate soon follows.

Except that is not how it works with the humans. They do not feel the bond as Tavikhi do. It must be earned. I bring forth an image of my mate. She is the smallest of the shefira's tribe sisters—not even reaching my chest—with short straight hair that is pale at the base, but soon turns dark. Her eyes do not match any color I have ever seen on Tavikh. I recall the fear in them, and it makes me wonder if my mate belonged to the part of Earth that was not wealthy. If she had no one to take care of her, how did she survive?

While I know the mate bond between Tavikhi brings an immediate sense of belonging and affection, I feel a sense of loss that it did not come to me. Zander said from the moment he touched London, he felt the pull toward her as though a cord connected them. As though his soul light was reaching out. I have not spoken to Zydon, but I will guess that same pull connects him to Remi.

All I can think about is the fear that glowed brightly in Maeve's eyes when she looked at my face. I run my fingers over the scar that travels across it. Is she appalled at my appearance? I growl and rip my hand away. It does not matter what she thinks. I already know that she will not accept a mating between us. Perhaps that is why I do not have affection for her. Deeka is preparing me for rejection. It is not the first time I have faced it.

Pushing the female's image away, I roll to my side and bring my furs up to my neck. The cold season is fully upon us, which means we must continue focusing on our food stores as well as hide stores. We used most of it to rebuild the dwellings destroyed during the Krijese attack. In the morning, I will go back to training the younger warriors and continuing their lessons to make them better able to hunt and fight.

I close my eyes and ignore the faint tingling that remains where my mating marks have appeared. Although it has never been heard of, neither has a mate rejection, perhaps in time they will fade and return my skin to its former color.

The scent of kokrra from the central fire wakes me. I lie a moment longer breathing it in before opening my eyes. The first thing I see are the darkened mating marks lining my arms. Memories of last night return. Of the celebration given for Zedam and his mate. Of the healer's tent. And of colliding with the small human female that is supposed to be my mate.

I raise my arm, turning it one way and the other, to study the darkened marks. It might be wishful thinking, but I almost see my baba's markings within my own. If only I felt the way about my mate as he did about his own. With a sigh, I lower my arm and rise from the furs. I quickly wash and put on a fresh pair of leg coverings. My belly roars like a hungry luani as I make my way to the central fire.

The sun has not fully risen, and my breath smokes the air. Few people are awake this early, but before long, there will be the sounds of the village coming alive. An elder as well as a female and one of the lesser injured warriors tends to the fire and the morning meal, preparing it for the rest of the tribespeople.

I fill a vessel full of warm kokrra without the shurup nectar many enjoy and take a seat. The quiet mornings are my favorite part of the day. It allows time for reflection and peace before it is interrupted with the chaos of village members wandering around. Of kits yelling and chasing after one another. Of warriors sparring, and the crash of metal against metal and wooden staffs against wooden staffs. It is the time of day when my baba and I would sit together, and he would tell me stories of his hunts and of the weapons he made.

Beyond the scent of the morning meal is the smell of cold dust. Within a lunar cycle it will fall from the sky and blanket all of our territory. It was my nene's favorite season. She said the cold dust settled in order to put all the beautiful things the warm season brings to sleep so when the time is right, they will return even more beautiful. How will the humans fare when the cold dust rises to our knees?

I glance out over the village. At how it has grown with the addition of twenty-one humans. Although they number sixteen now, after the Krijese attack. Of the five humans killed, one had been a young boy and his baba and nene. The entire village mourned the losses and celebrated their lives. From where I sit, and although it is halfway across the village, I have a direct and perfect view of the tent that contains my mate. Movement from it sharpens my attention and my muscles tense.

The hide door flaps open and I sigh. It is the healer's apprentice. Sage. Before last night I did not know her name or my mate's. I had no interest in knowing the names of any of the humans aside from our shefira and that was out of respect for our shefir. Although London is proving to be as strong in spirit and mind as Zander told me. Remi as well. She is brave, fierce, and determined. It had been an honor to craft a sword for her. She is a worthy warrior who is eager to learn and improve her fighting skills. Her strength may not be in body, but she is smart.

I do not know much of my apprentice yet. Many times, I bite back harsh words, but I am reminded of when my baba was teaching me his craft. Although I was a kit making mistakes, while she is a grown female, she is still just learning. I also see the potential in her. There is genuine interest behind her constant questions. She does not ask them all just to annoy me. So I bring forth all the patience I am able to and guide her.

Kyler says his apprentice is a fast learner. She is also using some of the herbs and plants he is teaching her about to craft some type of balm for herself and the other human females. I know many things about my mate's tribe sisters and yet nothing at all about her.

Although I know she is afraid.

The hide flap rustles again and this time it is Remi who exits. Followed closely by the shefira. Why are neither of them sleeping with their mates? The two embrace and go their separate ways; Remi toward the training arena and London toward the tent she shares with the shefir.

I have finished eating and still holding my empty vessel, yet I wait for another female to exit the tent. Moments later, yet another female—Alanda—carrying several woven baskets approaches it. She pats the hide and speaks, but from this distance I cannot hear what she says. After setting the baskets on the ground, she moves the flap and steps inside. Many beats of my heart pass when the hide door is opened and Alanda steps out.

I hold my breath.

Another beat, and there is my mate.

CHAPTER 6

I step outside and shiver. How in the world am I ever going to survive the cold season? I'm always freezing. Last night, with the fire going and all five of us huddled together was the first time I'd been comfortable. It got cold back in New St. Louis, but most of my days were spent in a hot factory. My walk back to my place was cold, but I didn't live far and in my tiny studio I was able to keep warm with the blankets my mother had made when she'd been alive. It helped that I was right over the boiler room.

"Did you and your tribe sisters enjoy your sleeping celebration?" Alanda asks as we head toward the bizele bushes to harvest some of them.

We didn't get much sleeping done, but I'd had a surprisingly fun time and it kept my mind off...other things. Of course, the minute I woke up, those other things were the first to pop into my head. I focus back on my friend and her question. "We did, thank you. This one was spur of the moment, but next time we'll plan ahead, and you can join us if you'd like."

If Tavikhi could blush Alanda would be doing so. She has been almost painfully shy around us, mostly just when London's about though. When it's just Alanda and me working together, Alanda is a lot more talkative and outgoing. I don't suppose I could intimidate anyone.

"I would very much enjoy that. You honor me, Maeve."

"You're our friend— our tribe sister—too."

We reach the bizele crop and Alanda passes me one of the baskets we use to carry the fruit. "You remember how to tell if they are ready?"

I nod. "If the root attached to the bush has turned orange." While that isn't actually how she described it, that's the way I remember.

"Good."

Knowing exactly what I'm looking for, I set off. The bushes are arranged in a pattern that is easy to follow without getting lost or trying to figure out if I'd already been past a certain section. I carefully check each piece of what us humans have started calling not-a-peach since it looks nothing like one, despite its taste, and put them in my basket if I feel like they're ripe enough.

Supposedly before the cold dust comes they should all be ready and the field will be empty until the warm season comes and the crop returns. I smile at the words 'cold dust' for some season. It definitely sounds a lot more fun than snow. Not that either of them are fun, but if I have to call it something, I like using cold dust. It's the perfect name for it.

I pick more bizele than I don't and soon my basket grows heavy. Making my way back to where Alanda left our other two empty baskets, I drop off my full one and pick up the next and return to where I'd left off. Some people might think fruit picking is a boring and tedious task, especially doing it alone in the quiet morning before most of the tribe has risen. Not me. After nine years of working in a loud factory where there's so much chaotic machinery that hisses and whirls and snaps, I enjoy the solitude. Normally.

Today, I don't like it. Because it gives me time to think and the only thing my brain is thinking about right now is… him. Of all the Tavikhi warriors, Benham's the largest. Not only in height, but build. He towers over the other warriors who have to be almost seven feet tall and his muscles are huge. No doubt from his blacksmithing. He could probably kill me with a single slap. Or wrap one hand all the way around my neck and squeeze. My airway tightens just thinking about it. David choked me once when I wouldn't stop crying. For a moment, while my vision had gone gray, I thought he was going to kill me. I learned to shut up after that.

Trying to keep my attention on my chore, I quickly fill the second basket and make my way back to where I'd set my first one. Except it's gone. I spin in a circle, my gaze circling with me while I check everywhere around the immediate area. I know this is where I put it. Alanda's empty one is still sitting right here. She steps out from one of the aisles with her basket and heads for me.

"Is all well, Maeve?"

"My other basket is gone. I set it right here before I went back to harvest more bizele, but now it's missing."

Her bony brow ridges shift. "No Tavikhi would take what was not theirs."

I let the insinuation pass that a human would, because I truly don't think she meant any insult by omitting them. It still doesn't explain the missing basket.

"Come. Let us take these to the food stores tent and I will ask if anyone has seen it."

Annoyed and confused, I let her lead the way. She comes to a halt shortly before we reach it and I almost run into the back of her. I move to the side to see what caused the hold up. There, lying in front of the door of our destination, is a full basket of bizele. *My* basket. What the hell?

"One of the hunters must have carried it here for you to help with the burden," Alanda says like it's a perfectly reasonable explanation.

Which, I suppose it is. I've only been in the village a few weeks and have only been helping her for one of them. Maybe this is a common occurrence that I just haven't seen yet. Still, it feels different. She walks to the tent and sets her basket down next to mine so she can draw open the door flap.

While I might appreciate someone carrying the load for me, what I don't like is that someone was so close, and I never even heard them. The bizele crop is all the way at the back of the village past the elder's tents. Anyone could be back here. Hiding. If the attack a few days ago is any indication—or the day Remi was bathing in the river—it's not the first time the Krijese have made it past the scouts. What's to say they couldn't do it again?

Up until now I didn't mind being back there with Alanda. Buddy system and all. But now all I can think about is the danger. Even if it doesn't yet exist.

"Maeve," she calls my name and I blink away the trance.

"Yeah, sorry, coming." I pass her the basket in my arms and she sets it inside the tent and I hand her the one on the ground.

Once all three baskets are inside the tent, we step out into the cold. "If you would like to wait here, I am going to go fill my other and ask who might have brought this one. When I return I will show you how we preserve these for the winter."

"Are you sure you don't want me to go with you? Four hands are better than two." I hold mine up and wiggle my fingers. Alanda looks at me like I have three heads.

"I will be quick."

Before I can offer up any protests, she dashes off. The wind kicks up and sends a cold chill running through me. I'm practically in the middle of the village. No one is going to do anything to me and it's got to be warmer in the shelter of the tent than standing out here. When another gust comes, I duck inside the food stores. The only light comes from a low torch staked into the ground where, in the other tents, a fire pit is dug.

I suppose they don't want it to get too hot in here and spoil any of the food. Even without an actual fire burning it's a few degrees warmer in here than out in the wind. I glance around and take note of the slowly growing supplies. Alanda doesn't know the exact head count of the village—perhaps seventy-five to a hundred is her guess—but there's a lot of people to keep fed for the next three months when hunting is scarce.

A scraping sound outside makes me straighten and the hairs on the back of my neck bristle. I wait for someone to enter, but the hide door stays closed. Why am I so jumpy all the sudden?

Another sound comes, but I remain alone. Alone with my thoughts. Which somehow automatically go back to Benham and the way he loomed over me last night. The way the torch light flickered across half his face. The scarred half. I don't know what caused it, but there's enough compassion inside me to feel bad for him. Although not enough to want anything to do with him.

Finally, after what feels like forever, Alanda says my name. I open the flap and step to the side so she can come in. I don't waste time.

"Did you find out who picked up my basket and brought it here?"

She shakes her head. "I am sorry, Maeve. Most of the village is only now rising from their sleep and leaving their tents. No one saw who did it."

It had to have been a tribe person. There is nobody else. But who? Could it have been Benham? I dismiss the thought the moment it enters my mind. Since no answer is going to miraculously appear, I try to forget about it.

"It doesn't matter. Now, you were going to show me how to preserve these?"

She roots around behind all the stored food and brings out two small knives, passing one to me. "First we must remove all the outer covering. Once that is finished, the fruit needs to be cut in small pieces. The covering is ground up and given to the elders to make their special brew we drink during celebrations. The meat is placed in a clay pot and cooked over the fire until all the juice has been removed."

Sounds easy enough. I'm assuming the 'special brew' is the alcohol that everyone was drinking last night. I wrinkle my nose, but try not to judge.

Alanda picks up one of the bizeles and gets to work. I do the same. We work quietly together, the only sound being the shearing of the skin. It's a lot easier, and quieter, than factory work. And it's nice having someone to sit with while we do it.

"You have not spoken of your mating with Benham," she gently breaks the silence.

Because I'm trying really, really hard to forget about it. "I kind of don't want to talk about it."

Alanda's yellow and purplish-black feline eyes blink like she's surprised. "I do not understand. A fated mate pairing is meant to be celebrated. Look at the shefir and shefira. Zydon and Remi. And now we have Zedam back with his mate. There may soon be kits again after too many seasons without them."

Children? Can humans even *have* children with Tavikhi? We're not the same species. "I know it's not the Tavikhi way, but some people don't want anything to do with a mate."

Alanda continues staring at me like she still can't understand how I could be one of those people. I don't mean to, because I hate talking about it, but I reach across and lay my hand on hers. "A man hurt me before. Back on Earth. It's nothing personal against Benham, but sometimes a woman loses all trust in men. And I know you're going to say he's a good person. But the friends of the man who hurt me said he was a good person, too."

She turns her palm up and clasps my fingers. "I am sorry that a male broke your trust. Tonight, I will pray to Deeka that Benham will show you he is a male worthy of putting your trust in again."

"That Benham will show you he is worthy."

Somehow those words help. He is going to have to do all the work to prove he's trustworthy. Except I haven't even seen him since last night. Maybe he has no interest in being my mate either. It would make things easier. I have no desire to hurt anyone. *What if he does want to be your mate? Then what?* Could he force me to be? The temperature inside the tent drops and a chill works its way down my spine. No. London said I had a choice. That no one would force me. Except London's as new to this planet and the Tavikhi as I am. Does she really know that to be true?

"Maeve? You are well?"

I force myself to look at Alanda and smile. "Yes, sorry. Thank you…um, for praying, I guess."

She smiles back like everything's great and returns to peeling the bizele. For the next hour that we work, I can't stop worrying that maybe London is wrong.

CHAPTER 7

BENHAM

I do not know what tempted me to follow Maeve to the bizele crop this morning nor carry the full basket of fruit to the food stores for her. Perhaps because I would help any of my tribe brother and sisters. Or maybe because it looked heavy and she is so tiny.

Several tribespeople linger around the central fire for the midday meal. I sit farthest from it on a small piece of carved fiku tree while I eat and observe. No one approaches me. Since the attack, more humans have finally joined the tribe for meals and have taken some initiative to help around the village. The elders are teaching some how to cure the hides, mend or make leg and chest coverings, while others help with preparing meals. I hadn't been able to withhold my surprise when a handful of males arrived at the training arena yesterday asking to be taught to fight. They were worse than kits and no one went easy on them. Best to figure out which ones will quit sooner rather than later.

The voices of several human females grow louder which draws my gaze. One is my apprentice, another the healer's, and the third, Maeve. She walks between but slightly behind the other two with her head down. Is her face always that pale? I admit to not paying any attention before. It makes her eyes appear even larger. She has a fur wrapped around her similar to the one last night.

I continue observing them as they help themselves to the leburin stew. Sage nudges Zara with her arm and laughs. My apprentice, in return, raises a single finger which only makes Sage laugh more. Maeve's lips curl into a small smile, but that is her only reaction. The three take their seats and eat while they speak to each other. None appear to have noticed me. My hearing is excellent, but the distance is too great for even me.

Why does Maeve sit on the cold ground between the two women and not on the wooden seat? I lift my gaze and Zara is staring at me.

I am done looking at the females. There is too much work to be done at my forge. I rise and place my vessel with others to be washed and walk away, only imagining that someone is watching.

I get the fire burning and while I wait for it to reach the right temperature, I organize my tools. Almost every one has been passed down from my baba. He taught me everything he knew about weapon making and fighting. There had been no greater warrior, aside from the shefir, than him. With every season that passes I miss him and my nene even more. The pain of their deaths is still almost as fresh as it had been five cold seasons ago.

Light footsteps approach, which means it is Zara. If it were a warrior there would be no sound. She enters the stoned off area that has served as the village forge for countless seasons. With the hill at its back and surrounded on all sides by a wall, it is protected from the winds.

"I'm here," Zara announces with something she calls a wave, as though her presence went unnoticed. "What are we working on today?"

Since I finished the set of daggers Evren asked for, there are no urgent needs. Although when I checked the weapons store yesterday its stock of arrows could be replenished. I gather a long, narrow piece of the metal we get from one of the tribes on a nearby planet for trade and bring it to the stone surface where I work. Zara moves closer and watches as I place one end into the fire to heat.

"So," she draws out the word. "You and Maeve, huh?"

I nearly lose my grip on it and turn to glare down at her. She is entirely unaffected by my look.

"There is no me and Maeve."

Zara's gaze drops to the mating marks on my arms. "I think those say otherwise."

"It does not matter what they say. Only what I say." My attention returns to my work.

She is silent after that. Far too silent. Every turn of the sun, she has been non-stop speaking or asking questions about what I am doing. She has told me of her life back on Earth, and after hearing from Zander how their people are divided, I realize she must come from the side that has much wealth. As the silence lengthens, I finally glance down at her.

"So you're rejecting her?" Zara jerks back as though I have offended her somehow.

"I am rejecting no one." It is Maeve who rejects me.

She tilts her head in that way she always does while her mind is working something out. "Then why haven't you even tried talking to her?"

Ignoring her question, I check the metal's color to test its readiness. "You are here to learn, not speak."

"Learning and speaking aren't mutually exclusive. You should know by now I'm perfectly capable of doing both at the same time. It's one of my many skills. Scratch that, it might be my only skill." Zara chuckles.

Grabbing my tool, I grip the metal stick and turn it to even out the heat. "Do you want to learn?"

"That's why I'm here, isn't it?"

I turn my head. "Then learn."

When she doesn't say anything else, I face the fire again. The end of the stick glows brighter than the flames. I remove it and place it on the stone. With my hammer in hand, I pound the end and keep pounding while turning the stick until a shape forms. I heat it again and pound more.

"You still didn't tell me what you're making," Zara says over the sound of the pounding.

"Arrowheads."

"Oh, cool. How do you make the tip pointy? That thing's flat as a pancake." She gestures to it.

I do not know what a pancake is. "I will heat it and then use a tool to curve each side until they overlap. I keep heating it and curling it until one end is narrow while the other end widens to be placed over the wooden stick that is the arrow. One it cools, I will use another tool to shape the narrow end into the pointy part as you say."

As Zara watches, I heat the 'pancake' once again until it is the shape I want and then I start bring the edges close until they overlap. More heat and more overlap. It is a long and tedious process, but finally it is curled into the desired shape. I heat it one last time, break it off the long stick, and chisel at the narrow end.

Once it is complete, I hold it up for her. "That is how you make an arrowhead."

Zara's eyes widen with excitement. "Can I try?"

I pick up another long metal stick and hand it to her. She glances at me and then back to the metal before approaching the fire. I have given her scraps to practice on over the last few turns of the sun. This is the first time I have offered her a real project. She is careful and thoughtful as she tries to remember the steps I shared. I have to assist many times, but only until she regains her rhythm. It takes until the sun has nearly touched the hilltop before Zara completes an ugly and unusable arrowhead.

She holds it up with pride. "This is the worst arrowhead I've ever seen, but holy shit, I actually made it. I think I know the things I did wrong too, so I can do better next time."

"It looks similar to the first one I ever made when I was a kit. You will improve over time, as I have."

Her face turns the color Zander said indicates shyness. "Thank you."

"We have been at this long enough. I can smell the evening meal from here. Go and eat. I will see you back here after tomorrow's midday meal."

Zara nods and fists her arrowhead. She reaches the entryway of the forge and twists to look back at me. "Maeve has been through a lot of shit. Bad shit. She'd be pissed if she knew I said anything, but be patient with her. Most of all, be kind to her. She deserves a decent guy. One who carries a heavy basket full of fruit for her, even if she was unsettled when she found it missing and didn't know who'd done it."

She takes off before I can reply. Not that my tongue can form words anyway. What kind of 'bad shit' has my mate been through? And I had unsettled her? That had never been my intention. Quickly, I douse the flames of the forge and put away my tools. Once I am sure there are no embers left, I make my way to my own tent to wash up.

I am at the central fire before any of the shefira's tribe sisters. I take my food to my regular seat while I wait for them to arrive. More tribespeople come, but not the one I am waiting for. The evening meal is when everyone gathers for a meal and conversation. It is also when Zander usually addresses any issues that arise. I am almost finished eating when I spot them. As usual, the shefira and Remi lead. Their mates can't be far behind. Zara and Sage are next. Maeve trails all of them, but I am happy to see Zedam's new mate walking beside her.

The females get in the short line that has formed to be served their meal. They have maneuvered in a way that puts Maeve in the center. Like they are her protectors. I rise from my seat and head toward them. The closer I get to Maeve the more my skin tingles and grows warm where my mating marks are. My tail thrashes and I work to keep it still.

Remi turns to speak to one of her tribe sisters and her gaze shifts to me. She nudges the shefira next to her and London whirls halfway around. Almost as one, the other four turn their attention my way, but my eyes remain on Maeve. She takes a tiny step in London's direction. Barely big enough to notice, but I do. I notice everything. Her rapid breathing. That flare of…unease in her eyes before she glances elsewhere and tucks her head.

I stop far enough away to hopefully ease any further nervousness at my presence. While tradition says my first greeting should be to the shefira, it is my mate who is the most important female at the moment. Even though she will not meet my eyes, I speak to her anyway.

"I took your basket to the food stores. I merely wanted to assist. My apologies, Maeve, that I did not let you know and if I caused you any worry. It was not my intent." I lay my fist over my heart, bow my head, and walk away.

Whispers meet my ears and stares follow my retreat, but I continue away from the central fire until I reach my tent. I grab the torch from outside and take it in with me. Once it is mounted in the ground, I kneel in front of the chest that contains my nene's and baba's few remaining belongings. There is a round stone in which I carved—poorly—an image of a ketri when I was only a kit. Nene said it was her most prized possession. I set it to the side and continue withdrawing items until I reach the bottom and find what I am searching for.

I take out the leather wrapped item and carefully unfold it. Lying in my hand is a beautiful chest covering with tiny crystals that reflect the firelight and make them sparkle like the stars in the sky. Along with it is a leg covering with the same crystals sewn along the bottom. It had been my nene's. She had it specially made after she and baba became mates. They had their own private mating ceremony and this was what she wore.

Although my nene was small for a Tavikhi, she was still much taller than my mate. Yet I picture Maeve wearing this for our own ceremony. She would look beautiful in it. Except I doubt she will ever want to.

CHAPTER 8

I stare after Benham in a weird state of shock. So it *had* been him. How did he know I'd been worried? I hadn't said anything to Alanda. In fact, the only people I told about my mini freakout were my friends. I suppose it doesn't matter, since I'm still processing his apology.

"That was nice of him," London says. "To tell you he's the one who did it and had only been trying to help."

Turning back to the fire, I tighten my grip on the bowl I'm holding. "Yes, it was."

Zara, who's on the other side of me, puts her hand on my arm. "What has you worried?"

I jerk my head in her direction. "Who says I'm worried about something?"

She drops her head toward her shoulder and widens her eyes. "Mae, no offense, but you're almost always worried about something. It's just how you are. A worrier. There is nothing wrong with it. We all have our thing."

Zara's right. Except I didn't used to be a worrier. "I guess I'm just worried I'm going to be forced to be mated to Benham before I'm ready. *If* I'm ever ready."

Remi leans around London. "No one's forcing you to do anything. I won't let them."

"*We* won't let them," London adds firmly. "If I'm the shefira of the village, then I'm going to have something to say about it. You can guarantee that Zander will regret every second of his life if someone tries to force you."

"What will I regret, and who is forcing someone to do anything?" the shefir comes from behind London and wraps his arms around her.

She turns and pokes him in the chest. "You'll regret making Maeve mate with Benham."

Zander pulls back and straightens to his impressive height that already towers over all of us. He still isn't as tall as Benham. He looks at me. "I swear on my honor that no one will force you to do anything."

"Thank you." For as long as we've been standing here, more and more tribespeople have arrived, and they're staring at us. Whether because we're holding up the line or for curiosity's sake. Either way, I'm ready to get my food and sit away from them all looking at me. "We should probably keep moving."

We finally all get our food, and by that time, Zydon and Zedam have arrived for their mates, leaving Zara, Sage, and me to sit together. The three mated couples are cozy together and talking amongst themselves while Sage is telling Zara about the balm she's trying to make out of paste and oils and whatnot. I suppose I'm included in the conversation as well, but I never really have anything to say. Sitting here, watching all of them, makes me miss the time on the ship together. We were a team, the four of us.

I quickly finish my meal since I'm feeling a little sorry for myself. "If you guys don't mind, I'm going to go. My stomach is a little…"

"Do you need one of us to come with you?" Zara move like she's going to stand.

I wave her down in a sudden rash of irritation. I'm a grown woman who doesn't need anyone to walk me back to our tent. I don't know who I'm more annoyed with. Zara for asking or myself for giving her a reason to. "No, I can make it there alone."

"Okay, if you're sure."

I get to my feet and dust off my butt. "I'm sure."

Avoiding looking at anyone, I set my bowl with the other dirty ones to be cleaned and head for my tent. Before I reach it, though, I take a small detour until I come to a stop in front of another one. I take a deep breath, tighten the fur around my shoulders, and smack my hand on the hide flap that serves as a door. The silent seconds stretch, and no one answers. I hit it again, this time a little harder.

Finally, there's a rustling sound and the flap is pushed open. Reflex makes me take a step back as Benham fills the whole space. My stomach lurches with the movement.

"Thank you for helping me today. I appreciate it." I get it all out before I second-guess my decision to come here. "Anyway, that's all I wanted to say. I'm sorry for bothering you."

I hurry and turn away.

"You were not bothering me," Benham says softly making me stop and slowly face him again.

He's still standing inside his tent, which eases some of my nerves. The firelight behind him puts everything in shadows, but in the fading light of the day, I can still make out the dark lines that mark his skin. A reminder of what they mean. My hands grow clammy and my mouth dries up taking with it anything else I might say. I haven't been alone with a man—a male—since David.

"Would you like to come inside?" Benham asks.

My head rattles fast and I clutch the fur around my neck. "No." The sound of my voice echoes it's so loud. "Sorry, I mean, no thank you."

He continues standing there with his tail swishing side to side. Staring. Waiting. I suppose because it would be rude to close the door on my face. *Do something.*

"Um, would you like to take a walk?"

"A walk?" Those bony ridges over his eyes shift. "Where are we walking?"

I wave my hand around in a general direction. "Just, you know, around the village."

Benham takes so long to answer, I'm about to tell him never mind and run and hide in my tent. My muscles tighten, but he finally nods. "Yes. I will walk with you. Give me a moment please."

He disappears back inside. He's only gone for a few seconds and the door opens and he steps out carrying a large fur. I didn't think the Tavikhi got cold. It's already freezing and they're all still running around half naked. At least the hunters and warriors are.

"That fur is not enough to keep you warm. Here." He holds it out to me.

I blink. He brought it for me? Why does that make my chest flutter? Slowly, I reach out. My fingers brush against it and I almost gasp. Oh my god, it's so soft. I slide off the fur I've been using as a cape and stick it between my knees while I throw the other one over me. The sweet, pungent scent of firewood mixed with cocoa tickles my nose. I have to hold back a sneeze. It's so big it hangs to my shins. I lift my head to look at Benham.

"This is way warmer than my other one. Thank you."

He nods. "It is the hide of the very first luani I ever helped take down when I was a young warrior, perhaps only fifteen cold seasons. My blow was the killing one, so I took its fur as my prize."

Now that it's around me, I'm not sure what to do with my smaller one, so I tuck it under my armpit. "I'm ready."

Together, we walk. I'm extremely aware of the male beside me, although he keeps a comfortable distance between us. I don't feel crowded at all.

The light given off by the central fire shines bright in the darkening sky, and every once in a while, it's visible when we pass the various tents that make up the village. A light breeze brings with it the scent of burning wood and meat, along with the voices of those still lingering around it.

The silence between us is a little uncomfortable, but I'm not ready to break it. I still can't believe I tapped on his door in the first place. A guy some goddess says is my mate. My husband basically. I can't help the shiver that runs over me.

"If you are still cold we can return."

I shake my head. "No, I'm fine."

We pass a few humans returning from the central fire heading toward their tents. They stare as Benham and I walk by. I can't help but notice the way they look at him, with quick side glances as though making sure he's staying where he is.

Is that how I look at him?

"Do you miss your Earth?"

I jump at the broken silence. "Not really. There might be a few good memories, but there are more bad ones. After my parents died, it got a lot harder. I was alone with only a few friends." I glance over at Benham. "I'm not sure how much you've been told about Earth, but where I came from, you didn't have much. I had to earn enough money to pay for everything, and the work was hard. Long hours with very little pay. I'm surprised I lasted as long as I did."

"I no longer have my baba and nene either. They have been gone for five cold seasons, but the pain of their loss is still strong."

Five years. "That's how long ago my mother died as well. Not a day goes by that I don't miss her. My father as well, although he died several years earlier."

We wander past the healer's tent, and the memory of the other night when I crashed into Benham comes back, along with my reaction.

"I'm sorry for how I reacted." I point in his direction and wag my finger. "You know. To that."

He dips his head. "You do not have to apologize. And you have nothing to fear from me. I will not force you into a mating. We can both continue as though this did not happen."

I should be relieved, right? And I *am*. Except.... "That hardly seems fair to you."

"There are many things in this life that are not fair, Maeve." He points out a little sternly. "It is not fair that our parents are dead. It is not fair that the Krijese have killed so many of our people. It is not fair that humans have had to leave their homes and travel to an unknown planet. It is not fair that there are many worthy warriors who may never get a mate. I have learned to live without things being fair and will continue to do so."

We come to a stop, and I realize we're back in front of my tent.

Benham fists his chest and bows. "Thank you for the walk. I enjoyed it."

He turns and leaves, his tail flicking almost erratically. *Say something. Stop him.* But I don't. I stand there—watching him—until he disappears behind another tent.

I step inside. Zara sits on her pallet rolling a hunk of metal in her hands. She looks up and scrambles to her feet.

"Holy shit, where have you been?" She smacks my arm. "London and Remi are out looking for you."

"I was out for a walk."

She stares at me. "A walk?"

"Yes."

"Alone? You don't ever walk alone."

I'm not sure why I want to keep the time I spent with Benham private. But I know she'll harass me until I tell her. "I wasn't alone. I was with Benham."

Zara gapes. "Benham? Are you serious?"

My cheeks heat. "You're making it sound weird."

"Are you kidding? This is awesome. C'mon." She tugs on my arm, pulling me down to her pallet. "Tell me everything."

I tighten my fur around me and the faint hint of cocoa hits me. Crap. I still have Benham's fur. Another realization comes to me. Not once on our entire walk was I cold.

"Earth to Maeve." Zara snaps her fingers in front of my face. "Tell me about your walk. No, don't. We should wait until everyone gets here. Eloise was going to stop by later, too, for a game of Pebbles."

"There's nothing to tell. Really." I ignore her side-eye. "I went to his tent to thank him for helping me, and I asked if he wanted to go for a walk. That's it. See? No story."

"I've never seen that fur you have wrapped around you. It's way bigger than any of ours." She quirks her lips like she's daring me to make something up.

The door flap swings open.

"We can't find—!"London snaps her mouth shut. "There you are. Are you okay? She's in here," she says over her shoulder and steps all the way in.

Remi enters right behind her. "Christ on a cracker, Maeve. You freaked us all out. We thought someone had kidnapped you."

"Maeve was on a date," Zara says smugly.

Both London and Remi's jaws drop, and I'm about to burst into flames. "It wasn't a date."

"It was a date."

"It wasn't—"

"Enough, children," London scolds and looks down at me. "Who was this not a date with?"

Zara opens her mouth and London jerks her arm up with her index finger pointed to the sky and Zara zips it. I sigh.

"I went to thank Benham for his help today. We ended up going for a walk and now I'm here. That's it."

London and Remi take a seat next to us, and we form a circle like we used to on the trip here. I've missed this.

"Does that mean you've accepted the mate bond?" London asks.

"It means we walked around the village and talked a little. You guys are my best friends, and I love you, but I don't want to talk about this anymore."

"Sorry, Mae," Zara says and her posture deflates.

"Yeah, we're sorry," Remi adds. "We'll keep our mouths shut, but if and when you do want to talk about it, you know we'll be there for you."

I reach over and squeeze her knee. "Thank you."

"We just don't want to see you get hurt," London says. "We love you, you know."

"I know." My shoulders straighten and it feels weird to not make myself smaller. "Now, I thought Eloise was coming and we were going to introduce her to Pebbles. And where's Sage?"

Zara jumps up since her bed is closest to the door. "I'll go find them."

"We need it to be warmer in here." Remi gets up and puts another log on the fire.

Except I'm already warm. I press my nose against Benham's fur, and that same cocoa scent I keep smelling is buried within the hide. It reminds me of him. Is this from his own bed?

I draw it tighter around me and take in another deep breath.

CHAPTER 9

Benham

I lie in my furs, the dark sky still holding onto the last remnants of the night before the sun crests the horizon and replay last evening. Nothing surprised me more than Maeve tapping on the entrance to my tent. Except her asking me to go on a walk. I have never walked anywhere without purpose before. Although I suppose the purpose of this one was for her to…. Actually, I do not know her purpose.

She does not have to tell me she does not want to be my mate. I already know, and despite her courage walking with me, there had still been fear in her eyes. It was in the way her gaze darted to me often as though keeping me in her sight. It had also been in the stiff way she held herself. And yet, she did not outright reject me. In fact, she talked of fairness. As if that is important to her. But what is fair of forcing a mating with someone who fears you?

No prayers to Deeka have passed my lips since the Krijese killed my baba and nene. What goddess would allow that to happen? Perhaps this is my punishment for forsaking her. Giving me a mate who rejects the bond that is supposed to bind us for life. I have never had the desire for a mate. Even less so after being orphaned. I have been a I fool to not understand the power of the bond and how a single touch changes everything.

Growling, I throw back my furs and rise. After quickly washing and donning clean leg coverings, I exit my tent and head for the central fire. Today, I join the hunters, instead of training with the other warriors. Zydon can take over for me unless he and his *keeshla* are heading out as well. Few tribespeople are out this early. Only hunters who are gathering weapons from the stores before they leave.

I serve myself a helping of oriz. While it is similar to kokrra, oriz is made from a different type of grain with a richer taste and texture. Both are filling and easy to prepare for the number of tribespeople those working the fire have to serve. Kokrra was my nene's favorite meal, although she sweetened hers with shurup nectar. She once said it was comfort food and reminded her of her own nene, and she would eat it every morning if she could. Perhaps she is who I get my love for it as well, although every morning is more than I would like to eat it.

I take my regular seat and eat. The scent of the fire fills the air, but beneath it is a hint of cold dust. There is still half a lunar cycle before it should start falling and blanketing the planet. More hunters slowly arrive for food, finish quickly, and sets off for the front gate. If I don't want to be out there past the midday meal, I should also get going.

After I discard my eating vessel by the fire, I walk back to my tent for my weapons. I place my belt around my waist, slide my sword in its sheath, and attach several daggers. Instead of my spear, I slip a satchel containing arrows onto my back and carry the bow outside.

Around me, tribespeople are spilling out of their tents. I pass one on my way to the front gate and Talek comes tumbling through the entrance of his. He runs over and walks beside me with the kind of excited, restless energy I associate with him.

"You are going hunting, Benham?"

"Aye."

"My baba said I can go with him today. May we join you?"

I have a fondness for Talek. My apprentice reminds me of him with her incessant chatter and endless questions. Similar to her, the kit asks important ones that will help him improve as a warrior and a hunter.

"Get your weapon."

Despite my gruffness, he grins broadly and rushes back into his tent. Several moments later he steps out with his spear. Following him is Samik, who has a sword slung across his back and a matching, but much larger, spear in his own hand.

"Greetings, Benham. Talek has said we will be joining you on your hunt today," he says with caution in his tone as though gauging how I will respond.

I nod. "Greetings."

The three of us pass through the front gate, guarded by Evren and Rojtar, who salute us on our way out. A swift breeze rustles the bari filled field before us and the branches of the forest trees sway and dance. With it comes the sweet scent of lulebore and the occasional sound of small ground animals rustling through the brush and the snap of a twig every so often.

"What are we hunting today?" Talek asks keeping his usually loud voice tempered.

"A sizable herd of dhibani on a hillside not far from here," Samik replies with a swift glance in my direction.

"Then let us search them out."

We head in the direction of the hills. Talek follows in his baba's exact footsteps as we make our way through the tall bari field he can barely see over. I keep my eyes on the trail along the base of the hills, watching for any sign of the Krijese who have made their home within the trees that climb up the side of them.

"Is this where our enemies live?" Talek asks.

"Until they prove otherwise, the Krijese who reside within the hills are not our enemies. They are merely people seeking a new life where they will not starve." Not once in my entire thirty-eight warm seasons would I have thought a peaceful tribe of the people we once called enemies could exist. We will remain cautious and vigilant in any encounters we may have with them, but for the moment, there is a peace between our tribes.

"Katem said he overheard Zydon report there are kits in their village. I have never seen a Krijese kit before. Are they as ugly and fearsome as a grown warrior?" Another question from Talek.

I breathe in patience. "I have never seen one of their kits either, so I do not have an answer for you."

"Do they have mates like the Tavikhi?"

Samik and I exchange a glance, and he answers his kit. "They do not mate in the same way we do. The gods they worship do not provide them *keeshlas* as Deeka provides us."

Talek appears thoughtful while we travel the path. His baba has moved to the back to keep the kit between us. My gaze shifts from the trail in front of us to each narrow passageway that splits the hills and travels upward as we go by it. I do not want to get caught unaware if we are attacked from behind, although I trust Samik to guard our backs.

"Why have we not celebrated you and your mate, Benham?" Talek says. "Ow. What was that for?"

I glance over my shoulder. The kit is rubbing the top of his head and looking back at his baba who stares fiercely in return.

"Because my mate hasn't accepted the mating bond between us." The fact stings a little, and I do not understand why.

"How can that be? Your mating marks appeared." He sounds genuinely confused.

Samik glances at me with a hint of worry and an apology in his eyes, as though he fears I will sharply reprimand the kit. Talek has never heard of such a thing before. Only the stories that have been passed down from ancestor to ancestor about how a single touch triggers the mating bond between two Tavikhi. About how the bond is so strong that one can not live without the other. It is not easy to understand why the same doesn't happen between a Tavikhi and a human.

I stop on the path and turn to look down at him. "A mate is not something to be given like a possession. Mates are a blessing. They are two beings brought together through fate. Except that humans do not feel the bond the way Tavikhi do. There is no soul light that shines from within them guiding them to us. We must find a way to share our soul light with them, which isn't always possible."

His small ridge brows shift together. "Do I have a soul light?"

"All Tavikhi have one," Samik responds. "It is ignited when Deeka places your *keeshla* in your path."

"What if my mate doesn't have one?"

That would only happen if his mate his human, and just a small handful of human kits live in the village. All but one of them is male. It is possible Talek might have a mate amongst the few female Tavikhi kits, but there is no way to guarantee it.

"If she does not, then you will find a way to share yours with her."

"But what if it isn't possible, like you say? Does that mean that I will have a mate, but she will not accept the bond?"

I lay my hand on his shoulder. "I do not have an answer for you."

With nothing more to say, I walk away while Talek and his baba continue talking. It does not last long and then all is quiet. I have my doubts that this will be a successful hunt. Not because there is no game to find, but because my mind is not where it should be. Three of our fiercest warriors have all managed to share their soul light with their mates. Would it really be impossible to share mine with Maeve?

"Benham," Samik says quietly. "There. Along that cliff, where the trees thin."

I lift my gaze toward the hills and spot what he has. A small herd of dhibani grazing in a narrow clearing, their hide helping them to almost blend in with the trees surrounding the area. We will need to pin them between us before they scatter into the trees or farther up the cliff-side. Their feet allow them to climb the rocky surface and stand on narrow ledges that would not hold a warrior.

With a few hand gestures, Samik and Talek break off from me while I continue forward to cut the dhibani off on the far side of the clearing. I make my way up one of the passageways between the cliffs and navigate through the trees, taking care with each step, until I locate where the dhibani still graze. I mimic the call of a mellenje and Samik echoes it.

Just through the other side of the trees, I spot the other warrior and the kit at his side who holds his spear at the ready. Being careful of any noise, I slowly withdraw an arrow from my satchel, nock it to my bow, and draw back the sinew cord. I take careful aim, breathe, and release it. Just as it hits its target, Rasik and Talek rush from their spot with a war cry. I drop my bow and unsheathe my sword as I charge forward to join them.

Talek's small spear pierces the side of one and it stumbles. Samik is there to quickly end its pain with his own spear. One of the largest dhibani with thick horns barrels toward me with his head lowered. I spin out of its way, but I am not fast enough to avoid the tip of its horn as it jerks his head. It slices me across the leg. Blood runs, but I ignore the pain. With a quick twist, I manage to ram my sword into the dhibani's side. I withdraw my weapon and stab again making sure to aim for its heart.

The beast collapses at my feet and doesn't move. Sounds of fighting have ceased, and I turn to search for Samik and Talek. The herd of dhibani have scattered and all that remain are the three we have taken down. I lower myself to one knee beside my kill, ignoring the stinging pain in my leg, and bow my head.

"Thank you for the food and warm hide you will provide our people. We honor you."

I rise and perform my prayer ritual for the other two beasts. Samik and Talek approach.

"Excellent job with your spear." I nod at the kit.

"Thank you." He points to the ground near the fallen dhibani. "Why did you kneel?"

"The dhibani do not choose to be killed, so I thank them for their unwilling sacrifice to provide meat and a warm fur for our people." I hoist the animal over my shoulder. "Come, let us take our bounty to the village."

Samik follows my lead, and although it is nearly too big for him, Talek does his best to carry the third. I limp back into the trees to retrieve my bow, and the three of us make our way down the hill toward the village. The temperature has fallen significantly in the time we have been gone and our breath smokes the air. We have to stop many times when the kit's load becomes too heavy, but he brushes off any attempts to take the animal from him. I do not blame him. When I was his age, I too wanted to prove myself as a hunter.

I tune my senses into our surroundings. The air around us is quiet. Too quiet. We reach the path at the opening of the passageway. There are no sounds of footsteps, but my back tingles as though someone is watching it. I remain on alert as we walk the path and then cut through the bari field, but everything is still. A flash of metal near the closest hill catches my eye. I stiffen and concentrate on the spot. Finally, I spot a lone figure in the shadows.

He's unmoving, and from this distance I cannot tell if he is Krijese or not. The only other people on this planet are the

Njeri. At least that we have encountered. If he is one of them, he is a long distance from his village. I keep my eyes on him as we exit the field and enter the forest that leads to our village. Even though he made no aggressive moves, my instincts are telling me not to trust him.

Samik gives a mellenje call, which is echoed back, and we finally leave the forest into the open field before the main village gate. With each step we take I become more aware of the pain in my leg. It is not the first time I have been injured, nor will it be the last, so I continue ignoring it.

"Come, let us take these to the tanning tent so they can be stripped."

Several kits come racing over to inspect Talek's kill. Excited chatter comes from them all as he relays how we brought them down. Several females and one of the lesser injured warriors greet us and we pass off the dhibani to be cleaned.

"It might be best to see the healer about that cut." Samik gestures to my leg. "You have lost much blood."

"I will take care of it." I leave him and head for my tent.

It is within sight when Maeve approaches. Her eyes travel down to my wound and her face pales. "Are you okay?"

"I will be fine."

She falls in line beside me but maintains more than an arm's length distance between us. No matter the distance between us, my mating marks grow warm and tingle along my skin. It is a somewhat unsettling sensation.

"That doesn't look fine. There's a lot of blood. Don't you think you should go see the healer?"

We reach my tent, and I pause in front of it. "Thank you for your concern. I will clean it and apply some of the healing salve I have inside."

To my surprise, she lifts her chin, looks directly at me, and straightens her shoulders. "I'll help you, but the hide flap has to stay open."

"You do not have to do that." It is clear she is uncomfortable with her offer.

"Please let me before I lose my courage."

She is brave, my little mate. I still have not discovered what the 'bad shit' of her past is, but someone has hurt her. I draw back the hide that covers the entrance and tie it so the interior of my dwelling is entirely exposed. First, I remove my arrow satchel, and next, my sword belt. With both in hand, along with my bow, I step inside and cross to my weapons chest. I do not ask Maeve if she is coming in. It will happen in her own time.

CHAPTER 10

MAEVE

I'm pretty sure I'm about to throw up, but I swallow it down, because I'm the one who offered to help Benham. All day, while working with Alanda to harvest some of the herbs from the large garden, I have done nothing but think about this whole mate thing. When she and I finished, I made London walk around the village with me while I observed how the males treated their mates. While I know they all say none of the Tavikhi, including Benham, would hurt us, words don't mean anything.

Is there such thing as a platonic mating? Like maybe he and I can just be friends. We could take walks together and tell each other how our day went. Or hang out by the fire during meals. But that would be as far as it goes. No husband-wife stuff. While I'm slowly coming to realize

Benham might not be quite as scary as I thought, I'm not ready for anything else, and I don't know if I will ever be.

Clinking sounds come from inside and I shake off the haze. I take one slow step inside and another, but that's as far I can make myself go. My feet are rooted firmly in the ground of a tent that looked a lot bigger from the outside. With Benham in here it's gotten smaller. *Way* smaller. My hands shake, and I clasp them in front of me to try and make it stop. He's put away his weapons and stands at a table placing a cloth inside a basin I assume is filled with water.

Why did I volunteer for this? I'm not a nurse. I have no idea what I'm doing. I've seen enough of my own blood because of David, but can I handle someone else's? Benham picks up the basin, and in his other hand is a really big knife. What is that for? God, I am so far out of my element. His gaze darts to the pallet on one side of his tent that I've done my best to ignore, but he doesn't head toward it.

The only other place for him to go is a chair near the firepit. It's going to be too hard to doctor his wound sitting.

I flail my arm in the direction of his bed. "Just go lie down. It'll be easier."

Benham doesn't reply. He calmly walks—limps—over to it and sets the basin on the ground and the knife next to it. When he finally lies down, I can almost breathe again, even though the tent doesn't feel any bigger now that he's no longer standing. It's just as suffocating as it had before.

"You do not have to do this," he tells me a second time.

Before I turn tail and run away as fast as I can, I take a step forward. And another. And a third. Until I'm standing over him. Was his bed always this far from the door? *It's fine. The door is open. Anyone walking by can see in here. He's lying down.*

As if that could stop him.

Shut up.

I lower myself to my knees next to the basin. "What's the knife for?"

"You will need to remove my leg covering from around the wound," Benham says as though it should have been obvious. How else am I going to clean and bandage it?

My hands tremble even harder as I reach for it. I graze the hilt with my fingers and yank them away. "You better do it."

"Maeve." That's it. Just my name.

I shift my gaze to him. He's staring up at me with those intense yellow eyes and they penetrate me as though piercing my soul.

"I trust you."

Three simple words. Yet they resonate inside my head. Benham trusts me. Which means I need to trust myself. I take a deep breath and reach again for the knife. Keeping my eyes on his leg, I slide the tip of the blade through the already present tear and cut his hide pants from just above mid-thigh to ankle. There's a trail of dried blood down the entire length of his leg and the wound still oozes.

"What happened?" I wring the excess water out of the cloth and carefully clean his skin, avoiding the actual wound for the moment.

"A dhibani horn."

I wince and dip the cloth back in the basin to rinse the blood out before attending to the long, and what looks like a pretty deep slice. Benham doesn't flinch, though it has to hurt. I can't help but study the other scars that cover his chest and wonder how he got them. Especially the one on his face. The shiny puckered scar runs along the entire side of it and disappears into his hairline. I can't imagine how painful that had to have been.

"There is a salve in the chest over there." Benham gestures with his chin. "You can put some of it on the wound."

I'm not an expert, but I don't think slapping some salve on this thing is going to cut it. Still, I stand and go to the chest. Sure enough, there's a round wooden container near the top. I open the lid, just to make sure.

Man, this stuff stinks.

I come back to sit next to him. "Are you sure this is going to be good enough? It looks really bad."

"It will leave a scar, but the salve will help heal it."

"Would anything not let it scar? Maybe there's something else that Kyler or Sage has." Why do I keep pushing?

"Maeve," Benham says my name again in that soft tone that makes me look up at him. "I wear my scars proudly. They are a sign of strength. That I am a worthy opponent. Even if it is only against a dhibani."

It's so self-deprecating, I manage a small smile. "I'm sorry."

"You do not have to apologize. I am honored that you care."

My smile falls. Not because I don't care, but because I do. Even though I haven't accepted the mate bond, Benham has still been kind.

"Right, yeah, sorry," I fumble the container and rip my gaze from his to yank the lid off. "Let me get this stuff on the wound."

I hesitate and glance around me. All I have is a bloody cloth. *This is so unhygienic.* I dip my fingers in the goo and carefully spread it over the cut, making sure I cover every inch. Once I'm satisfied, I wipe the excess off on my pants and replace the lid.

"Now that I'm finished and looking at it, I realize how much of his leg is exposed, and if I open the hide any farther, it's not just his leg I might be seeing.

I jump to my feet and move several steps back. My cheeks are flaming hot. Completely on fire. I need to dump a cold basin of water over my head. "Um, sorry, yeah. Do you need a bandage?"

"Thank you, but I can bandage it myself."

"Okay." I keep my eyes averted. "Is there anything else I can do while I'm here?"

"That is all. Thank you for your help."

I bob my head up and down and walk backward toward the entrance. "I…I hope you feel better."

Before Benham can say anything, I bolt out of the tent and nearly crash into Zara.

"Whoa, are you okay?" She clasps my arm to steady me. "I heard Benham got hurt? I was coming to check on him. Wait. What were you doing in there? Why is your face all red?"

Her lips tighten and a fierce light enters her eyes. "Did he do something to you? I don't care how big he is, if he hurt you, I will ram one of those daggers of his right through his heart."

"No, no," I rush to get out. "I'm just being me. Benham didn't do anything. I helped clean and doctor his wound. That was it. I just weirded out for no reason. I promise."

Zara slowly loosens her shoulders, and the tightness around her mouth eases. "You swear?"

I look her straight in the eye. "Swear."

"Good, because I'd really hate to have to murder my boss."

She'd probably try, too, and get herself killed in the process. "No murdering needs to take place."

"If he ever does something to hurt you, I won't hesitate."

Although I know it makes Zara uncomfortable, I give her a huge hug anyway, squeezing her tight. "Thank you for being my friend."

"Yeah, yeah." She awkwardly pats me on the back and I let her go.

I chuckle. "You're going to get used to us hugging you one of these days."

"God forbid," she deadpans and I glare at her. "Anyway, since I found you and since I doubt Benham is heading to his forge today, London and I are going to hold a session for the kids if you want to come along. She's trying to teach them how to read and write. Although I have no idea why considering there aren't a whole lot of books—meaning none—available to any of us. But she wants to do it, so I guess we are, since she's the chieftess or whatever."

For a second I'm tempted, because it will occupy my mind. But there's something else I should do. "Why don't you go ahead?"

"All right. Catch you at dinner then." Zara walks away but turns and walks backward with a smirk. "Oh, and if you see Benham again, let him know I'll be at the forge tomorrow."

She winks and keeps walking. My cheeks heat, because that's what I'd been thinking of doing. He missed the midday meal, and he shouldn't be walking on that leg. Before I question and overthink every decision I've made in the last two days, I quickly head to the central fire.

"Hi, excuse me, is there anything left over from lunch? The midday meal, I mean."

The male looks me over. "You are Benham's mate?"

Flustered, I stutter. "No—yes—no—I don't know." I snap my mouth shut and breathe. "I'm his friend and I would like to take him a meal if there is anything left over since he missed it."

He stares at me a minute longer, before putting some leftover meat from an animal I don't want to know about and a few root vegetables on a wood plate and hands it to me. "For your friend."

I take it from him with thanks, ignoring his sarcasm, and slowly make my way back to Benham's tent at the far side of the village. Except I make a pit stop first at mine and fold up the large fur I forgot to return. When I make it to his home, the hide flap covering the entrance has been closed. I smack it. He didn't leave, did he?

"It's me, Maeve. I brought you some food."

Several seconds pass before I hear anything inside. The hide moves and there Benham stands with his brow bones raised. He's already put on a clean pair of pants. "You did not need to bring me anything."

"I know I didn't. But I also wanted to return the fur you loaned me." I lift my arm the fur is draped over.

"That was meant for you to keep," he says. "As a gift. I know humans get much colder than Tavikhi."

A gift? For me? Except for the few Christmases when my parents were able to save enough money, no one has ever given me a present before. The stuff David gave me were nothing more than bribes.

Benham gave me a blanket so I didn't get cold. One special to him. I tug it close to me. "Thank you for the gift."

He bows his head. "You are welcome."

"Here." I practically shove the plate at him in a nervous gesture. "Your food."

Benham takes it from me careful not to touch me. "My thanks."

We stand there, neither of us making a move to leave. I rock back on my heels. "Right, well, I guess I won't keep you then. Thank you again for the fur."

Feeling awkward, I hurry away, clutching the blanket tightly to me, and go search for London and Zara. I'm not really sure what I thought would happen when I took Benham food. I guess I'm trying to get to know him better.

It's the *why* I don't understand.

CHAPTER 11

Benham

It has been two turns of the sun since Maeve brought me the midday meal. Two turns of the sun since I have seen her at all. She has been absent from the central fire each day and even my apprentice has been unusually quiet. Is Maeve sick? I should ask Zara, but I have not. Because I do not want to make things uncomfortable for my mate if she is well but has decided she no longer wants to speak to me.

Not that I have hoped she might accept the mate bond. Hope is a fickle thing. But I had thought we could become friends. I admit I've missed her soft, quiet voice, even if she did not use it often.

Zara is working on another arrowhead. I have paused while crafting mine to offer her some assistance on occasion, but otherwise, she has been making them herself. It is still ugly and useless, but it is less ugly and less useless than her first few attempts. She will succeed. I have never seen someone work as hard as she has. When she approached me, I did not truly believe she would last long. But she has surprised me. There is no hint of her giving up.

I heat my metal once again and curl the sides tighter until they are nearly sealed. It goes cold, so I heat it once again and then chisel the tip.

"Are you even going to ask if she's okay?" Zara speaks up.

I stop what I am doing and do not pretend I do not know who she is speaking of. "No one has said anything about one of the humans being ill, so I assume she is well."

She stares at me with her lip curled in a snarl. "You would *know* if she were well if you'd bother to come and ask her. But no. You're just ignoring the fact she exists after she put herself out there to try and be your friend."

"I am not ignoring that she exists. I did not want to contribute to the 'bad shit' she has been through by forcing my presence on her."

Zara continues staring and staring. I try not to shift like a kit being reprimanded. Finally she shakes her head. "You're a chicken shit."

"I am not a…chicken shit."

"Do you even know what that means?" She glares. "It means you're a coward."

I bristle in offense and my tail thrashes wildly behind me. "I have battled hundreds of Krijese and taken down many dhembe as well as a luani. I am no coward. These scars prove it."

"Yet you haven't made a single effort to check on Maeve. How many times has she had the courage to come talk to you? To step inside your tent—alone—and care for your wound. You have *no idea* what that took for her. Just because her scars aren't visible doesn't mean she doesn't have them. And you can't even be bothered to stop by to make sure she's okay or even just to say hi. It's like you don't even care about her, and yet she's supposed to be your mate?" She turns her back on me and jabs her metal stick in the fire.

Shame fills me, because Zara is right. Maeve is my mate. Neither of us chose this. Deeka did. I have never wanted a mate. Even less so after my baba and nene were killed. Yet the goddess brought one to me anyway. One who asked me to take a walk with her despite her fear of me. Who braved coming into my tent to tend my wound. Who brought me a meal because she did not want me to be hungry.

I set down the arrowhead and my tools and leave the forge. As I walk through the village, humans and Tavikhi alike move about together, each intent on their destination. The laughter and playful yelling of the kits fill the air. I spot two human kits amongst them. The humans are slowly becoming true tribespeople. I finally come to a stop in front of Maeve's tent and slap the door.

It opens, but it is not my mate.

"Did you need something?" Sage asks.

"I have come to check on Maeve. Is she well?"

She turns away, mumbling what sounds like "took you long enough", and the hide flap slaps down over the entrance. I continue standing there staring at it as though with my mind alone I can make it move. It remains closed.

I am sure no one is coming, and I'm about to turn away when it is opened. My mate is wrapped in the luani fur I gifted her but appears well.

"Yes?" She tightens the fur around her and appears even smaller than usual. This is also not my Maeve. The fear in her eyes has been replaced with hurt. Did I put it there?

"Are you well?"

"I'm fine."

I study her. She says she is fine, but I do not think that is true. "Have I done something to anger you?"

Maeve releases a sigh and her shoulders drop. "No, Benham, you haven't done anything to make me angry."

Zara's words return to me. "I am sorry for not seeking you out sooner. I did not think you wished to see me again."

She jerks. "Why would you think that?"

I do not want her upset with her friend for speaking to me of something Maeve would not want me to know. "I know that you fear me and I did not want to cause you any distress by coming to your tent." To my own ears it is a flimsy excuse.

"Well you caused me distress by *not* coming. I thought we were starting to become friends."

"We were—are. I do not have many friends. None that are female. I do not know how to act."

"Friends check on each other. And they don't wait two days to do it. Since you never came by, I thought *you* didn't want to see *me* anymore."

Slowly and carefully I reach up, but stop before touching Maeve's face to give her the chance to tell me no. When she does not, I lay my hand along her jaw. It is the first time I have touched her since the night my mating marks were triggered. That same warmth heats my skin, and my marks darken farther. There is a shifting sensation inside my chest. "I am sorry, Maeve. I did not mean to hurt you. If you can forgive me, I would like us to be friends."

Maeve does not draw away, but she does not lean into it either. Not wanting to push her any further, I lower my arm to my side and wait for her to choose. I will not blame her if she says no.

"Friends take walks. I suppose we could go for a walk since I've been cooped up in here for two days."

"Were you ill?" The guilt presses harder on me if she was. She should have someone to take care of her.

"Just really exhausted. The nights here are shorter than they are back on Earth. Remi and I are apparently the only ones having a bit of a time adjusting to the difference. So nothing a little more sleep won't cure."

Relief fills me that it is not anything more serious than that. "Perhaps only a short walk then so you can come back and rest."

"I'm feeling a lot better today. Let me grab my shoes, and I'll be ready." Maeve ducks back into the tent and before long, she steps outside still wearing the luani fur.

We walk away from her tent with no destination in mind. I gesture to the covering she continues to use. "Is that keeping you warm?"

She draws it tighter around her and sighs, but it sounds like one of pleasure. "This has been the best gift I've ever received. It's kept me warmer than anything else I've tried. Thank you again."

"I am glad."

A kit runs past and I step out of his way. Talek chases after him. I glance around at the village where I have lived my whole life. In only a short time, it has changed so much.

"How's your leg doing?" Maeve asks.

I touch it absently. "It is doing well. You make a good healer."

Maeve laughs and it settles deep within me. "I don't know about that. I've seen enough blood to last me a lifetime."

Her laughter fades and I glance down. She is looking ahead, but I do not think she is actually seeing anything. "I am sorry you had to see mine."

She blinks and gives her head a small shake. "Oh, I didn't mean that. I wanted to help, and the blood didn't bother me."

If it was not mine that bothered her, where has she seen too much? I want to ask, but I do not want her to recall any bad memories. Speaking is something I have never been good at. It is only something I do when necessary. It is no wonder I am having trouble making conversation. Maeve is not a hunter or a warrior.

"Are you enjoying learning from Alanda?" We pass the food stores tent where the two females have spent a lot of time.

"I am, actually. Back on Earth, we didn't have this kind of food. If you were someone like me, you ate protein bars. If you were someone like Remi or Zara, you had machines that made you actual food like a steak or cheeseburger. On rare special occasions, those of us who lived on the bottom tier might get to taste some of it. But only if we were lucky, which didn't happen often."

I try to picture food from a machine. How is it cooked if there is no flame? How do the kokrra grains become soft if they are not soaked? "It does not sound like a place I would like to live."

"I didn't like living there much either."

"Is that why you came to Tavikh?"

We come to a stop in front of Maeve's tent. She is quiet for many beats. "I came because I had no other place to go. Staying on Earth was no longer an option. Wherever that spaceship was heading is where I was going. I didn't even care where. So long as it took me someplace far away."

"Yet it brought you here." To my planet.

She lifts her gaze to me and smiles softly. "I guess it did."

Of all the planets in the galaxies that Maeve could have landed, it happened to be this one. Perhaps Deeka guided her to me and me to her. For the first time since the death of my baba and nene, I offer a prayer of gratitude to the goddess.

"I am glad you are here."

"Me too," she almost whispers.

My gaze drops to Maeve's lips. I have seen the mouth touching Zander and Zydon do with their mates. Until now it did not look appealing. But I am beginning to understand the appeal.

"May I mouth touch with you?"

Her furry brows shift and a crease appears between them. But then they lift and her large eyes grow even larger. "Oh, you mean kiss."

Is that what the mouth touching is called? Kiss? "Yes, I would like to share this kiss with you if that is all right."

She chews on her lips and her throat moves as she swallows. Several beats pass before she slowly nods. I do not dare move fast. As though she is a dreri frozen in place, I take care not to startle her. She is so tiny I have to lean down a great distance until I carefully and gently press my mouth to hers. The sensation is pleasant enough.

Sensing she has reached her limit, I rise to my full height. Her cheeks have turned the color of the manerrat berries. I take a step back and bow my head. "Thank you for the kiss. I will let you get some rest. But if you are feeling up to it, maybe we can take the evening meal together by the fire."

"Okay. Yes, I would like that."

"I will see you then." Before I beg for another kiss, I walk away and head back to my forge where Zara remains.

She glances up at my return. "It's about time you got back. I looked up, and you were gone."

"I needed to go see my mate."

She places her fists on her hips. "So *now* she's your mate?"

"Maeve has always been my mate. We are also friends and have come to an understanding."

Zara glares a moment longer before shaking her head. "She's always been a softy. If it were me, I would have made you grovel a little."

This does not surprise me. My apprentice is a fierce one. I am glad my mate has a friend like Zara to protect her. As I pick up another metal stick, I relive the mouth touching—the kiss—and I hope to do it again.

CHAPTER 12

Maeve

I stare after Benham. He kissed me. And I let him. I'm not sure which one surprises me the most. The minute he asked, my heart raced with a mix of fear and excitement. No one has ever kissed me so gently or briefly. It almost didn't even qualify. A mere brushing of lips. Yet, I felt it throughout my whole body.

A cold breeze blows my hair in my eyes. I tuck it behind my ear and go back inside the tent with Sage and the fire. There's a torch planted next to the center pit providing additional light and heat. She's sitting at her pallet working on the balm she's making for us to try on our skin and glances up.

"How was your walk?"

I take the seat I'd vacated when Benham showed up and go back to grinding the plant I offered to help with. "It was nice."

Even though I count Sage as a friend, I've known her the shortest amount of time. And none of us know what brought her to Tavikh. London either, for that matter, although knowing she's from the bottom tier like me, I'm sure she had a good reason.

"So you guys are dating, then?"

My immediate response is to deny it, but isn't that what we're doing? Going for walks. Eating dinner together. Those pretty much constitute dates. Not that I have much experience with them.

"I suppose maybe we are."

The only person I ever "dated" was David and that was more dragging me to parties at his friends' houses. He always introduced me as an afterthought and never as his girlfriend. Just "This is Katherine." Then he'd ditch me for the rest of the night to get drunk. I'd go find a quiet place to sit until he came back and told me he was ready to go. We'd go back to my place, he'd come into the room I rented, have sex with me, and leave.

"I'm happy for you Maeve. You deserve a good guy," she says and tips her head back down while she works on adding an oil from some plant to the mixture. It has a flowery earthy scent to it. I study her.

"It's just you and Zara left, I guess. Do you think you're the mate of one of the warriors?" Zara has already said she's all for finding a mate, but Sage hasn't said one way or another about it and she's been on Tavikh the longest. Six months give or take.

"I don't know if I want one, although I suspect it won't happen after all this time," she says. "I mean, if we're all here because of fate or destiny or whatever, then what is Deeka waiting for? I've been on this planet for a while. I've been to this village countless times working with Kyler when I still lived in the human settlement before we moved in here. You'd think she would have put my fated mate in front of me by this point if I had one."

But if Sage hasn't touched anybody except for Kyler then she wouldn't know. How many warriors has she touched who've come into the healer's tent? There have been six in there since the Krijese attack on the village a week ago. Before that there were a couple other warriors she worked on. And none of their marks were triggered.

"Maybe she's waiting for something." It's a thought. Why else would she bring all of us here, if not to give us mates?

"I'm not sure what she'd be waiting for. I've been here this whole time." Sage sweeps her arm out.

"Maybe it's not you she's waiting on. Maybe it's the warrior. Maybe he's one of the younger ones and needs to age a few more years."

She snort laughs. "Great, Deeka is going to make me a cradle robber."

"Not *that* young." I chuckle. "Aren't there a few warriors that are nineteen or twenty? That's only, what six or seven years?"

"More like ten."

Oh. For some reason I've always thought she was closer to my age. "Still. Ten years isn't that much. Human men date and marry younger women all the time. Even ones more than ten years younger. Why does everyone make such a huge deal out of when it's the woman who's older?"

"Misogyny," Sage says without missing a beat.

"True. Earth has always been a man's world." Men get away with crap and people dismiss it as boys will be boys. No one cared what was done to me. Not just because David was rich, but also because he was a man. "Tavikh is different though. I doubt anyone would look twice if your mate is younger than you. They'll thank the goddess for yet another blessing."

"Yeah, you're probably right. I'm still not going to pin my hopes on anything." She reaches out for the mortar holding the plant I finished grinding up. I pass it over and fold my hands in my lap. For several minutes I sit quietly and watch her pour my plant remnants into her own bowl and stir it up.

"Can I ask you a question?"

Sage glances up at me. "Of course."

"What if I'm wrong?"

Her forehead creases and she tilts her head the tiniest bit. "Wrong about what?"

"What if I can't ever be more than friends with Benham? I'm still so confused about if I even want to be more. I'm clearly a terrible judge of character. It wasn't that long ago, I thought Deeka was punishing me." I pick at my cuticle. "He offered to forget all about his mating marks and we'd both go about our lives as if they didn't exist and never happened."

Sage completely stops what she's doing. "When did he do that?"

"The night he confessed to being the one to take my basket of bizele. I left the evening meal to come back here, but I wound up at his tent first to thank him. He said it before we went for our walk."

"Has he mentioned it again since?"

I shake my head. "No."

"Can I ask *you* a question?" She leans forward and rests her elbows on her folded legs.

This feels like a trick. "Yes."

"Why didn't you take Benham up on the offer? He gave you the perfect out."

I gnaw at my lip. "Because it isn't fair to him."

"What about you? Is it fair to you to be given a mate you didn't even want?" She claps her hands over her ankles.

Before that whole dark period of my life, I'd always hoped to find a nice guy to fall in love with. The kind of love my parents had. I wanted someone to snuggle with at night. To talk with. Laugh with. Maybe have a kid with.

"He kissed me. Benham, I mean."

Sage sits up and her eyes widen. "When?"

"After our walk." I point to the door. "Outside the tent right before I came back in here."

"Wow. And?"

My cheeks flame. "It was nice. There wasn't any tongue or anything. He just brushed his lips across mine."

"Did you like it?"

I press my fingers to my mouth, where there's still a slight tingle. "Yes."

"Then maybe you should follow that feeling. Trust your gut if it's telling you something." She picks up her wood bowl and goes back to stirring her concoction.

My gut says Benham might be special. That maybe I don't have to be afraid anymore. I get to my feet and bend to give Sage a hug. "Thank you."

She pats my arm with a small laugh. "You're welcome."

I hike my blanket up higher and leave the tent. The wind has picked up and my hair flies everywhere. Cold air manages to sneak past the neckline of the fur and skate down my back. I shiver, which kicks me into gear. I walk past the healer's tent and the food stores, my gaze straight ahead and intent on my destination. In no time, I reach Benham's tent and smack the door. He doesn't answer. I slap again and wait, but still nothing. Maybe he's at the forge.

Gathering my bearings, I head in the direction I think it is. I've never seen it, but Zara has told me all about it. The strong scent of burning fiku wood hits me as does the sharp metallic clanging. I maneuver around a tent and there it is bordered on two sides by a stone wall with the mountainous hill at its back.

My steps slow. I'm not sure of my welcome. I don't want to disturb Benham's work, but I'm also curious about it. I feel like he knows so much more about me, aside from the real reason I'm on Tavikh, and I don't know nearly as much about him. I haven't been a very good friend. Bolstering my courage, I stop at the entrance and look inside.

Zara is the first person I spot. She's bent over a long stick and using some tool to curl the metal tip into what I think is supposed to be a conical shape. Her tongue peeks out between her lips as she works. The sharp clack from the other side of the forge draws my attention. Benham is slamming a type of hammer down on the tip of a similarly shaped conical piece, but his is much more obvious. With each blow that lands, a sliver of metal breaks off, forming a sharp point.

He smashes the hammer down again and rises, bringing the cone shaped piece he's holding with some tool up to his face. His eyes meet mine and he lowers his arm. I wave a bit awkwardly.

"Is all well, Maeve?" He sets down his tools and comes closer.

Zara stops what she's doing as well and her head jerks up. "Is everything okay?"

"Everything's fine. I didn't mean to bother either of you. I just came to talk to Benham for a minute." We just walked around the village talking. They're probably wondering why I didn't say whatever it is I need to say then.

But Zara's eyes widen knowingly and she darts a glance at her boss, whose back is to her, and over to me again. She grins in that self-satisfied way and comes around to the other side of the table from where she's working.

"I'll just leave you two alone." She walks past me on the way out and as she does she leans in slightly. "Don't do anything I wouldn't do."

I want to cover my face but keep my hands within my blanket. Finally, it's only Benham and me. He closes the last bit of distance between us, but still gives me plenty of breathing room.

"Are you sure you are well? What is it you need to speak with me about?"

Now that I'm here, my courage is slowly leaking out.

"Maeve?" He uses that same tone he did before and the sound of it is calming.

"I'm sorry. You probably have a lot of work to do. I didn't mean to interrupt."

Benham takes a single step closer, but no more. "Do not ever be afraid to seek me out if there is something you need. I am always available to you."

"Thank you. Would you mind if I stayed a little while and watched? I've been curious what it is exactly you do back here. Like that." I point to the thing he'd been crafting when I arrived. "What is it you're making?"

Benham glances behind him. "Zara and I are making arrowheads. Well, I am making arrowheads. Zara is…learning."

I bite back a grin. "I'm sure she'll get better."

He nods. "Aye, she will."

"I'm glad she found something she enjoys. We were all a little worried about her, but none of us have seen her as excited as she has been. She's finally found her calling, I think."

"I have no doubt that Zara will become a fine weapon maker." Benham turns part way. "Come. I will show you if you'd like."

He walks back to where he'd set down what he'd been working on and I follow. Between the warmth from the fire and the walls cutting off the cold breeze, it's not bad in here. I loosen my hold on my fur. Lying in stacks against a wall are long metal rods. He picks one from the top and sticks the end of it in the fire until it's bright red and then he gets to work.

I can't help but stare at the way his muscles ripple and shift as he moves his arms. Or at the near-black curling and climbing tattoos—mating marks—that line his leather-textured, purple skin. London says it's way softer than it appears.

"Benham?"

He stops hammering and gives me his full attention.

"Would it be okay if I…if I touched you?"

"Is that what you would like to do?"

No. Yes. Maybe. My hands shake and I clench and unclench my fists. "I think so."

"My Maeve," Benham says softly and hearing him call me his makes my stomach flip-flop in a weird way. "I would like nothing more than that, but I want you to *know* that you want to, not just think you do. When you can say yes without hesitation, then I welcome all of your touches."

I didn't expect that. What guy would turn down the offer for a woman to touch him?

Apparently this one.

I'm not sure if I should be mad or grateful.

CHAPTER 13

BENHAM

There is nothing I would like more than for Maeve to touch me, but I sense her hesitation. If she is hesitant, then she is not touching me for the right reasons. I cannot believe there was ever a moment after my mating marks were triggered that I thought I held no affection for my mate.

My soul light shines for her. It is so bright I do not understand how no one is blinded by it.

"Do you know you're probably the first guy who's ever turned down being touched by a woman?" She huffs and her breath is smoky in the cold.

"Being touched by you would be my greatest pleasure. But how can I enjoy that pleasure if my mate cannot say for a fact it is something she wants to do? If we are to ever become mates in truth, it is because you welcome me with no hesitation."

Maeve drops her head slightly. "Do you want to be my mate?"

I set down my tools and carefully step closer, pausing only long enough for her to put space between us. When she does not, I place my finger under her chin and slowly lift until our eyes meet. "I stopped praying to Deeka when my baba and nene were killed by the Krijese. Since you have come into my life, I have prayed to her almost nightly asking her to show you I am a worthy mate, because there is nothing I want more than to be yours."

Maeve's mouth opens on an "Oh."

I drop my arm to my side and return to my work. My mate has a lot to think about. I reheat my metal rod and, careful of where she stands, place the heated end on the stone table. Just as I reach for my hammer, a touch as soft and light as a mellenje feather brushes along my arm. I remain unmoving, not wanting to scare my *keeshla* away since she has become so brave.

The blunt-clawed fingers run over my skin, tracing the pattern of my mating marks, causing them to heat and tingle. The sensation heads straight to my cock and I grit my teeth to keep the hardness at bay, but it is difficult when Maeve touches me so gently. I do not know what I have done in this world to deserve a treasure such as her, but I offer another prayer of thanks to the goddess for this blessing.

My mate continues her exploration, pausing at each scar that represents the battles I have fought. I can recall every encounter and which beast or enemy gave it to me. What caused the scars that I cannot see inside my mate? Her soft touches climb upward, gliding over the flesh of my shoulder, until she reaches the one that mars my face. I may have dealt the killing blow to the luani whose fur drapes over my mate, but he left me with one more thing to remember him by.

Maeve traces the length of the scar up into my hair and threads her fingers through the length of it. It falls around me as she releases it. Unable to resist, I turn my head to finally look at her. She leans in close and her plush chest mounds press into my arm as she rises up and gently mouth touches—kisses—me. That same pleasant sensation runs through me, but it feels like something is missing.

There's a light flick of something against my lips and I realize it is her tongue. Is this something humans do? They taste each other? I part my lips and touch my tongue to hers. My Maeve is delicious. Since this is my first time touching tongues with anyone, I let her lead and teach me how to do it. She is tentative, as though testing it out, and then grows bolder.

Except she is too far away.

I wrap my hands around her waist and draw her close to me. It takes me a moment to realize that I am the only one still doing any tasting. My mate has gone rigid and trembles in my embrace. I lift my mouth from hers and slowly loosen my hold until I have completely released her.

Maeve's pale face is even paler, and her eyes are open, but it is as though she is not even seeing me.

Taking care not to startle her, I speak her name quietly. Once. Twice. Finally she blinks and is back with me. The human wetness fills up her eyes and fall down her cheeks.

"I did not mean to make you fear me again, Maeve."

She rattles her head side to side. "No, it's not you. It's me. I'm sorry for getting all weird on you."

"If I did something you do not like, I wish for you to tell me so I do not do it again."

"It wasn't your fault. And it wasn't that I didn't like it. I just wasn't expecting you to put your arm around me." She swipes at the wetness spilling from her eyes and loosens a breath. "I hate talking about this, because I want to forget it ever happened, but if we are going to be mates, then you deserve to know."

If we are going to be mates. My soul light dims a little, but that is not what's important now. Maeve and what just happened is. "You may tell me anything. I will always listen."

"Yeah, but sometimes things aren't easy to say or hear." She wraps the luani fur more tightly around her as though she has gone cold again. "Back on Earth I had a boyfriend."

"Boyfriend?"

She shifts. "Yeah. It's like a guy you date—go on walks with and eat a meal with—and hope to fall in love and get married. Mated."

I draw back. "You had a mate?"

"No, he wasn't a mate. He was just a guy I dated. A not nice guy. In fact, he was terrible. I hate him so much," she says fiercely. "When he would get mad—which was all the time—he would hit me."

If I could travel to Earth, I would find this *boyfriend* and I would kill him.

"That's not even the worst of it." Maeve laughs, but it is the one I do no like. "He's the reason I'm here on Tavikh. The last time I saw him, he…hurt me. Forced me."

He forced her to do what? I try to puzzle it out, because this is so clearly painful for her, and she has been caused enough pain. I will not add to it. She is afraid of me or *was* afraid. She did not want to be alone with me in my tent. She did not go stiff until I held her close.

"Aren't you going to say anything?" Maeve rasps. "Have you decided you don't want a mate who is damaged goods anymore?"

I reach for her hand, making sure I do not make any sudden moves. "I do not know what that means, but there is nothing about you that is damaged. You are brave and strong. You are also kind and generous and the most beautiful female I have ever seen."

"So you don't care that I'm not a virgin? I'm not sure if I'll be able to be a proper wife—mate—to you. Not after what he did to me. How could you want a mate who freezes just when you put your arm around her? What happens when you try to touch me in other places and I can't do it?"

A sudden knowing comes over me and I finally understand what my poor Maeve went through. I want to kill this male all over again. I cup her face in my hand and joy fills me when she leans into it. "Do you care that I have never touched a female?"

Her little nose wrinkles. "Of course I don't."

"What if I am not a proper mate to you? Because I am unskilled. Would you still want me for a mate?"

Maeve places her hand over mine. "You know it's not really the same thing, right?"

"Who we were before Deeka blessed us is not who we are now. Whatever happens between us is what we decide. I have gone thirty-eight warm seasons without touching a female and I expected to journey into the land of the goddess still having *never* touched a female. It does not affect my wanting you as a mate. I will always want you as my mate."

The water fills her eyes again and spills out. Maeve takes a tiny step forward and another until she is touching me. She puts her arms around me and lays her cheek against my abdomen. I stroke her hair to try and soothe her, but do not touch her in any other way. My mate needs to know that she can move away from me anytime she needs to and that I will not hold her if she does not want that.

Soon Maeve is done leaking water and releases me. She wipes away the wetness and takes in a shuddering breath.

"I wish I had come to Tavikh a long time ago and met you then."

"You are here now and that is what matters."

She glances around. "God, I'm sorry. You were busy working and I've disturbed you long enough."

"You are never a disturbance. I welcome your company any time. No matter what I am doing."

"Still, I should probably let you get back to making your arrowheads. Since Zara is…learning." Her lips twitch. "I'll see you at the evening meal, though?"

I nod. "Of course. I would very much like that."

"Me too." Maeve walks to the doorway and pauses to glance back. "I very much liked kissing you as well."

Before I can reply, she leaves the forge. I am looking forward to our meal together even more, which makes going back to work harder. We will have plenty of time to spend together this evening though. I return to my project and try to lose myself in my craft. When each arrowhead grows worse, I know it is time to stop. My mind is not here. It is already with Maeve. I set about smothering the fire and putting away all my tools. Once that is finished, I head to my tent to wash the dust and smoke from my skin.

I make it to the central fire before my mate. Jodah, who I have not spoken to in several turns of the sun, approaches. He crosses his fist over his chest. I return the gesture.

"Blessings on your mating," he says.

"Thank you."

"Evren and I spotted traces of a luani today while out hunting. We are going to search for it tomorrow and are looking for two more hunters to join us. Since you have faced one down before, your skills would be valuable."

As much as I would like to spend more time with Maeve, a luani would feed our people for many turns of the sun. Its hide would provide warmth through the cold season. "I will join you."

"My thanks." He glances past me and dips his head. "Your mate comes."

I turn and there she is with Zara and Sage. Our eyes meet and affection fills my heart. I clap Jodah's shoulder and cross the distance between my mate and I. My apprentice nudges Maeve with a questioning glance. My mate nods. Zara and Sage break off from their group leaving me with my *keeshla*.

My tail twitches with the need to wrap around her and draw her close, but I will not do so until she invites me. I stop short of her, giving her space. Only she does not take it. Maeve walks the last few steps closer until we are practically touching and tips her head back to look up at me. Her arms go around my waist yet again and she rests her head on me. I will carry the sensation of my mate pressed against me into my tent tonight.

She draws away, but only slightly. "I'm practicing touching. Is that okay?"

"It is more than okay. You may touch me any time you like."

Maeve glances away but returns her gaze to me. "Maybe you could try hugging me. But not too tight."

I have never been one for gentle. As a warrior and hunter, strength and power are honed from a young age. There is no gentleness when taking down a luani or dhembe. There is no gentleness when fighting against a Krijese. For my *keeshla*, though, I will be gentle. Always.

Slowly, I wrap my arms around her, keeping my touch light. For the third time, Maeve puts hers around me as well and lays her cheek to my skin. We stand near the central fire as tribespeople make their way in our direction for the evening meal, and yet I remain here with my brave mate in my arms. It is the best feeling in all the galaxies. When I feel her hold loosening and she draws back, I release her instantly.

"I did not hold you too tightly, did I?"

Maeve's cheeks are that pretty color, and her smile is sweet. She shakes her head. "No, it was perfect."

"Good." I straighten with pride and hold out my hand. "Let us eat."

She slides her tiny one inside mine and we make our way over to the fire and the large pots filled with stew hanging over it. Once our eating vessels are full we walk to the spot where I usually take my meals. I sit and leave room for my mate. She pauses, glances at the empty place, at the ground, and back at the spot next to me, before finally lowering herself at my side.

CHAPTER 14

I just stood in front of all the tribespeople present and hugged Benham. Yet sitting on the carved stump is what makes me feel vulnerable. Unprotected. Neither of which I should feel. The biggest warrior in the entire village is seated next to me. There is no one here who would dare hurt me. I'm coming to believe neither would he.

"May I ask you a question?" His voice is low like we're having a secret conversation.

I like that no one is near us. It's just Benham and me. "Sure."

"Why is it that you ate your meals seated on the ground?"

"Ever since I left Earth, I've been afraid. God, even before I left I was afraid. Afraid he would find me. Afraid another man would hurt me. But if no one can see me, then I'm safe. As stupid as it might sound, sitting on the ground where I'm somewhat out of sight, guarded by my friends makes me feel protected."

"I do not think that is stupid. We do whatever we can to protect ourselves. I am glad that your friends have made you feel that way. That no one will hurt you." Benham brushes his finger along my cheek. "If you will let me, I will also make sure that you are safe and protected."

I clasp his hand and hold it against the side of my face to breathe in the scent of smoke and cocoa. Finally, I release him so we can eat.

Sage catches my eye and she dips her head slightly almost in encouragement. London, Remi, and Eloise, with each of their mates, get their food and they all take different seats. I glance at the rest of the tribespeople sitting around the fire. There are more humans present than I recall ever seeing at an evening meal.

A sense of home and peace fills me. Here on Tavikh, there is no upper or bottom tier castes. No standing in a hot factory for hours toiling away for little pay. Here there is community. Friendship. Family. I don't think I understood how alone I've felt since my parents died.

"You have grown quiet. Well, more quiet. Almost as quiet as me," Benham says with a teasing lilt.

"I was just thinking."

"Would you share these thoughts with me?"

It's a question, not a demand. In fact, he's asked for my consent for everything. A kiss. A touch. He even let me decide whether or not to enter his tent when I basically forced him to let me tend his wound. As if I could force Benham to do anything. Still, he gave me a choice. And continues to do so.

"I was thinking about this place. Tavikh. The village. The people." *You.* "How less alone I feel by being here."

His scans the circle of people gathered at the fire. "I too have felt the loneliness. Especially after my baba and nene were killed. My heart has been missing a piece ever since they died." Benham turns his head towards me. "You have filled the spot that has remained empty these last five cold seasons. And now I do not feel so alone anymore."

There's a sharp crack in the wall inside my chest. With his kindness and tenderness, he is slowly chipping away at my defenses. I don't know that I can protect myself against it. I'm not sure I want to. No man—male—has ever looked at me the way Benham has. Made me feel the way he has. Not even David at the beginning. It absolutely terrifies me. More than anything ever has. And I don't want to be scared anymore.

"Could we go back to your tent?"

I'm not sure if I've surprised him with the request, because he does nothing more than blink. "Is that something you truly wish to do?"

"Yes." This time there is no hesitation.

Benham takes my empty bowl from me and deposits his and mine by the fire. He returns to me with his hand out. I reach for it and let him bring me to my feet. We leave the center gathering place and I can feel my friends' gazes following us. Our walk to the far end of the village is quiet, other than the fading voices of those we leave behind. The sun is almost behind the hills and one of the two moons is a third of the way to its peak.

We reach Benham's tent. He releases me, but only to pick up the torch from outside with one hand and open the flap of the tent with the other. It's built for his frame, so I don't even have to duck to step inside. It looks exactly like it had when I was here tending his wound. The trunks on the opposite side, the chair beside the banked fire, the table with water basin, and the massive pallet where he sleeps. He steps past me to add more wood to the pit and plant the torch in the ground beside it. It catches quickly.

A cool breeze blows across my back. I turn to find the flap tied open.

I walk over to loosen the tie to let the flap fall closed. For a second, I'm not sure I can breathe and then I inhale deeply and turn back to face Benham. He remains on the far side of the tent with his arms crossed. His eyes are unreadable.

Taking slow steps forward, I walk the entire length of his home until I stop directly in front of him with my toes almost touching his. The mating marks along his arms are just above my eye level. I reach up and gently pull them down exposing his middle. With a final step I lean into him, laying my cheek on his abdomen. He towers over me in a way that should scare me. His hand engulfs mine while we walked here. The same hand I had thought not that long ago would cause me harm.

"Will you hold me again?" I whisper against Benham's skin.

There's only a moment's hesitation before I'm wrapped up in his loose embrace. Too loose. I squeeze him tighter and as though reading my mind, he does the same to me. It's still loose enough that I could escape if I needed to. But I have no need to. I snuggle even farther into his warmth. I've never felt so safe and cozy before. Before my parents' death—before everything—we'd always been an affectionate family. I didn't know how much I missed that until now.

"Will you tell me something about yourself?" I've told Benham pretty much all there is to know about me, but I want to get to know him too.

"What would you like to know?" He voice vibrates through him and into me.

"Anything." Everything. "What's something you've never told anyone else?"

There's a brief pause as though he doesn't want to tell me or he's thinking about it. He strokes my hair and I love the way it feels.

"I have always been bigger than any other Tavikhi my age," he begins. "Even as a kit. I wanted to be the strongest warrior and the best hunter of anyone else. Djentar was Shefir before Zander. He was the fiercest of all of us. I learned everything I could from him. How to fight. How to take down a dhembe."

I don't know what kind of animal that is, but his voice is so soothing, I don't want to interrupt him to ask.

"When I turned fifteen cold seasons, we went out on one of the lasts hunts before the cold dust blanketed our territory. Djentar, my baba, Moshur—who is one of the elders—and I set out early one morning. The wind blew swirling the cold dust so hard that it was difficult to see through. We went high up into the hills where a few other hunters had spotted excrement from a luani a few turns of the sun before."

From Alanda, I figured out a luani is some kind of lion but twice as big with long, vicious claws and a mouth full of razor-like teeth. I shudder, picturing what it might look like, and Benham's hold tightens around me.

"We finally tracked it down. I could see its bones through its hide. The beast was starving. It looked up and our eyes met. I knew, in the moment, that I could not kill it. It was just trying to survive. But by then, it was too late. Djentar and my baba attacked first, followed by Moshur, while I remained frozen where I was. In no time, they wounded it, and I had to end its suffering."

My heart aches at the pain in Benham's voice.

"In a final attempt to save itself, it lashed out with a claw that sliced across my face. I should have felt anger or hatred, but I only felt pity. It was then I dealt it the killing blow and I spoke words of apology to the dead beast. I gave it thanks for providing us with its hide and with what little meat it had left. I never spoke of my hesitation to kill the beast."

I loosen the tight grip I have on him, and when I shift backwards, Benham's hands fall away from me. Although he's so tall, I rise on my tiptoes and cradle his jaw between my palms. I guide him down until he's bent enough at the waist for me to kiss him.

He shifts and moves and I move with him without breaking the kiss as he lowers himself to his knees and kneels in front of me. At this height, he's the perfect level. The light flick of Benham's tongue teases the seam of my mouth and I open for him. This is only the second time we've kissed this deeply, but he's a fast learner because I'm riding high on a tide of pleasure. I wrap my arms around his neck and meet the slickness of his tongue as they both tangle together.

Benham grips my hips loosely. Nothing more than that. It gives me the courage to take a tiny step forward so my breasts are crushed against his chest. A week ago I'd be panicking at being inside an enclosed tent with a male and today I'm kissing one. Maybe I can let down my barriers and push away my fear. I want so badly to be able to kiss my husband—and more—without worrying I'm going to freak out.

More than that I want Benham to touch me without the memory of anyone else's hands creeping inside my brain and ruining everything. I want to experience what it's like to make love, not just have sex.

There's a light pressure around my waist. In an instant, I know exactly what it is. I brace for the panic to hit, but it doesn't. Instead, I deepen the kiss and thread my fingers through the length of Benham's hair. It's so soft and makes me miss my own long hair. I don't know how long I stand there, with him kneeling in front of me, kissing him. Time has ceased to exist.

Breathless, I break the kiss and rest my forehead against the hard ridges of his. The harsh rasps of our breath mingle with the sound of the crackling fire that pops. Emotion clogs my throat and weighs heavily inside my chest. I don't want to let him go. Not while I've got this feeling of hope growing within my soul. Loud voices pass by outside and I finally lift my head from Benham's.

His cat-like eyes glow in the firelight, reflecting the flames behind me. I trace the scar along his face. The one the luani he couldn't kill gave him. What a kind heart my husband has. Another sharp crack slices through my walls. They teeters but don't fall. Something tells me they will, though.

CHAPTER 15

Benham

The most wonderful sensation I have ever experienced is having my mate in my arms. Maeve stares back at me with those beautiful eyes, and something inside them shifts.

"I very much enjoy sharing these kisses with you," I echo the same words she said to me when she left the forge. "Is my hold too tight?"

She shakes her head. "Not at all."

"This makes me glad, because I have discovered I enjoy holding you along with the kisses."

"I'd like to stay a little longer if you don't mind," Maeve says. "But I don't want you to spend the whole time kneeling."

It would make me happy to spend all my time with my mate. Even on my knees. "I will place some other furs down and we can sit."

I unwind my tail from her waist, although I wish to keep it there, and stand. From one of the chests, I bring out several more furs and lay them beside mine but keep space between them. Maeve walks over and brings them closer so both sets touch. She sits and pats my sleeping place next to her. The trust she is granting me I will never take for granted.

Once I am seated with my legs crossed, my mate turns to face me so her knees touch mine.

"This is the first time I have sat with a female alone in my tent. I am not sure what I am supposed to do," I confess.

Maeve laughs in the pretty way I love to hear. "The is the first time I have sat with a male alone in a tent. So, we're both new at this and we can learn together. I wanted to spend more time with you, just us together. Talking. Learning about each other. Is that okay?"

I move slowly as I reach out and take one of my mate's hands in mine. I trace the inside of it and she trembles. Next I move along the outside, running my finger over her blunt claws. Her skin is so pale against mine. I lift my gaze to hers. She blinks back at me.

"That is more than okay."

"Did you always want to be a blacksmith?"

My translator doesn't recognize that word. "Is that one who crafts weapons?"

Maeve nods. "Basically. A long time ago on Earth there were men mostly who would do things similar to what you do, although it wasn't always weapons they made. But they melted and crafted things from metal after heating like you."

Her question is not an easy one to answer. "For as far back as I can remember, my ancestors were these 'blacksmiths'. It is a tradition that has been passed down to every male born. I did not know of anything else to be."

"Do you like doing it?"

I pause to think about it, because I am not sure I have ever taken the time to wonder if I do it because it was expected of me or because I truly enjoy it. "I do. There is a kind of beauty in making something out of nothing. And what about you on Earth. What was it that you did?"

She expels a breath. "I worked in a hot factory where I stood sweating for ten hours a day making these stupid cover plates for the machines that made food for everyone in the upper tier. It was a thankless job that underpaid everyone, because they could. Jobs weren't always readily available in the bottom tier, so once you found one, you stayed there. Usually until you died."

How terrible life back on Earth was for the humans. It is no wonder they left their planet and came to Tavikh. "I am happy you are no longer in that place."

Maeve laughs a little. "You and me both."

"Did your nene also work in this…factory? Is it a tradition that is passed down to the females?"

"Definitely not." She shakes her head. "No, my mother crafted items from fabric. She would make clothes for people or fix stuff that was ripped and torn or needed to be resized. Similar to what some of the elders do. She also made blankets, but nothing like these furs."

"And you did not follow her in this crafting?"

"My skills in that area were sorely lacking I'm afraid," Maeve admits. "She tried teaching me when I was little, but everything I tried to make was a disaster. Which meant I had to find something else to do. Hence factory work. I started there when I was fifteen and I probably would have been there the rest of my life."

I send another prayer to Deeka for taking my mate away from that place and bringing her here to me.

"Do you wish for kits?" I snap my mouth shut, wishing I could take it back. Only because I do not want fear to seep into this special time together.

Maeve startles. "One day, I think. When I was younger, I used to dream of who I would grow up to marry and how many kids we'd have. But it was always just a vague thought. Until my parents both died. They loved each other so much and I wanted that same kind of love. I wanted to find someone I could fall in love with and have children with."

Her words settle between us. I want to be this someone she falls in love with and has kits with.

"What about you?" Maeve asks softly.

"If Deeka chooses for me to have kits, I will be the most blessed male. There have not been any kits born for so many seasons. Talek is among the last. But I have always had a fondness for them."

She flips her hand over and does to mine what I did to hers. With her gaze focused on where we connect, her tiny finger traces the inside of it and over the rough bumps that have hardened after so many seasons of holding and wielding weapons. Maeve turns it over and her finger glides along the back of it.

"You have such gentle hands," she says. "One of the first things that went through my mind after your mating marks appeared was how much you could hurt me with them."

Sorrow fills me that my mate would ever think I could do such a thing. But that is how the last male treated her. It is no wonder she feared me. I want to tell her that I will never hurt her, but words are sometimes not enough. All I can do is show her.

Maeve takes my hand and brings it close to her. When she places it on her chest mound, shock rushes through me. Tavikhi females do not have the plush mounds that humans do. I am unsure what to do so I keep still and wait for her to tell me what she wants. I will do nothing to make my mate fear me again.

"I just wanted to see if I could do it," she says, finally lifting her gaze to meet mine. "How it would make me feel."

"How does it feel?"

"Nice. Tingly."

Those are not the words I would use to describe it. *Bliss. Paradise.* The most perfect thing I have ever felt. When she removes my hand from her chest mound there is a loss inside me. Except she raises her chest covering and brings my hand back to her bare flesh.

I lied. *This* is the most perfect thing I have ever felt. I watch Maeve intently for her reaction. The moment there is any fear in her eyes I will stop touching her.

"You can touch me." Her voice is soft and quiet.

"Am I not already?"

She smiles and it is a truthful one. "I mean you don't just have to keep your hand still. But only above the waist."

"Are you sure this is what you wish?"

"Yes." Again, there is no hesitation in her answer.

I tenderly mold the plump mound with its hardened tip. My eyes do not leave Maeve's so I can see what brings her the most pleasure. I rub one finger over the swollen bead. A small shudder goes through my mate, but her eyes have gone dark and she makes a soft noise I can only assume is one of pleasure. I explore the slope, kneading it, and plucking at the rigid nub.

"What is this called?" I roll over it with a finger.

"The whole thing is called a breast and the hard center is called a nipple." My mate is breathless.

Breast. Nipple. I roll it again between my fingers and Maeve arches closer. "This pleases you?"

She bites her bottom lip and nods.

Bringing my mate pleasure makes my cock hard. It presses against my leg coverings and my mating nodes leak the fluid meant to excite our mates even more. "May I use both hands?"

"Yes."

I slide my free hand under her chest covering to touch her other breast with its hardened nipple. She is soft beneath me. I gently squeeze her mounds and soothe them with tender stroking. Are kisses also for breasts? I have a sudden need to know what my *keeshla* tastes like. What I would not give to see Maeve's body bare, but I will be satisfied with what she has gifted me. I will not take anything she has not offered.

"Can I touch you as well?" she asks.

"You may touch me whenever you like."

My mate's gaze darts away from my face and back. "You're kind of far away and my arms aren't as long as yours. Maybe,"—she pauses—"um, maybe we could try lying down?"

"Do you truly wish this?"

"I want to try."

My brave little mate. I bring my hands out from beneath Maeve's chest covering and shift until I am lying on my side facing her. She takes a deep breath and lies down as well so we are eye-to-eye. I reach up and push her hair back behind her ear.

"What do these colors mean?" I stroke the pale section closest to her head that abruptly turns dark.

She does not speak for a moment. "When my friend hid me from my ex while we waited for the ship bringing me here to arrive, she thought it best to try and disguise me in some way. So, we colored my hair brown and cut almost all of it off. My real hair color is blonde, which is the light color. As my hair grows again all the top will be blonde and the bottom part stays brown until I cut it off."

I have never heard of changing one's hair color. "Which one do you like best?"

"The blonde. That's what color my mother's hair was, and people always said we looked a lot alike. I thought she was beautiful."

If my mate's nene looked similar to her, she must have been, because there is no one more beautiful than my *keeshla*. "When you are ready to cut the dark color from your hair, I would be happy to do so, if you like."

"Thank you. And thank you for distracting me so I could get used to lying here with you."

Distracting her had not been my purpose, but I am glad I was able to. "You are welcome."

"I think I'm ready to be touched again. I mean, if you'd like." Maeve ducks her head and with my finger under her chin, I tip it up.

I lean closer and brush my lips across hers. She opens without hesitation and I slip my tongue inside. Since my mate enjoys kisses, then I will give them to her until she knows she is ready to be touched again. There is no doubt when Maeve returns to her tent, I will be stroking my cock while I am thinking of her. I deepen the kiss, sweeping inside to gather up all her flavor.

Warm hands land on my chest and slide over my heated flesh. My *keeshla* touches me like she did at the forge, exploring the hills and valleys of my arms. She draws back and licks her lips.

"Please touch me."

As before, I slide my hand under her chest covering until I reach her breast. It is still as plush and firm as before and I play with her nipple as she strokes up and down my arm.

"Wait, stop," she says.

I do so immediately and quickly remove my hand from Maeve's soft body.

She shakes her head. "No, that's not what I meant."

Before I can ask what she did mean, she sits up and lifts the chest covering up and over her head baring herself to me. She crosses an arm over her breasts and lies back down.

"It was in the way and didn't feel right."

"What about now?"

Maeve laughs softly. "Terrifying, but also kind of good."

"It is the same for me."

She blinks up at me. "What has you terrified?"

"You. The thought that you could fear me is terrifying. I do not ever want to give you reason to."

"It has been hard for me to trust my judgment about people." Maeve reaches out and traces the mating marks on my chest. "Sage told me I should follow my gut, and my gut says you would never do anything to hurt me."

"Never," I vow.

Her eyes stay focused on my chest and then she lifts her gaze to meet mine. "I know we were going to practice more touching, but do you think you could just hold me?"

"It would please me very much to do so."

Maeve scoots as close as she can get to me with her arms folded up and covering her chest mounds. Her flesh is chilled so I bring a fur up over us and embrace her. Her breath is warm against my skin sharply contrasted by the cold nose she buries against me.

"You smell like cocoa." My mate inhales deeply.

My translator does not recognize that word in our language. "This is a good smell?"

Maeve nods and her nose rubs up and down over my chest. "Cocoa is used to make chocolate, which is a sweet back on Earth. I've only ever had it once, but it was one of the best things I have ever eaten."

"I am glad that I smell delicious to you."

She laughs. "Me too."

There has never been a greater feeling than having my mate lying in my arms in our furs. I want nothing to disturb it, so I remain quiet and enjoy the peace that flows through me. Maeve must be content as well, because she remains still and silent until her breathing becomes even. I will let her sleep for a little while, since she has said she does not get much. My eyes close as well. I will rest for only a moment and then wake her so she can return to her tent before her tribe sisters worry about her.

CHAPTER 16

I haven't been this warm since before we arrived on Tavikh. The scent of the sweet pungent wood mixed with cocoa tickles my nose. Why does it smell like cocoa? There's no chocolate on this planet. I shift and register a heavy weight draped over me. A feeling of being trapped hits me and I breathe in deeply. That's when I realize a large hand is palming my breast. I stiffen. *Just keep breathing and think.*

"Maeve?" The hand is gone and cold air hardens my nipple.

Most of the tension in my body releases at the sound of Benham's voice. God, I must have fallen asleep. I open my eyes. The torch has gone out and the fire needs more wood so it's nearly dark inside the tent. I roll over to face him.

"Please forgive me," he says as soon as I'm all the way around.

I scrunch my forehead. "Forgive you? What did you do?"

"I did not mean to touch your chest mound without asking first. There is no excuse for it."

"Hey," I reach up and stroke his face. "It's okay. I'm going to assume you fell asleep as well."

Benham nods. "I only mean to rest for a moment."

"It's all right. I promise." As comfortable as I am, I should probably leave. I'm actually surprised I fell asleep in the first place. I hold the fur to my chest and sit up. He does as well. I glance over at him. "Thank you. For tonight."

"It has been my greatest pleasure."

I snatch up my shirt, and keeping the fur in place, slip it over my head. "Morning will be here soon, so I should get back to my tent."

"Would you like me to walk with you?"

When Zara asked me that the other night when I left the central fire and came here to Benham's tent, I'd been annoyed. It doesn't feel the same when he asks. I get the sense he's asking if I want to spend even just a little more time together. When she had, I'd gotten the impression she asked more because I needed a babysitter.

I lean over and kiss him. "Thank you, but you should get some more rest. It's not far. But I'll see you in the morning?"

"Jodah has asked me to join him and Evren on their hunt for a luani they may have found. We will be leaving before the sun rises. If we are successful, I hope to return before the evening meal."

My stomach twists. "Please be careful."

"I shall."

After one more kiss, I wrap my fur around me and exit Benham's tent to make my way to mine. Only a few torches are lit along the way making it hard to see in the dark. I'm rethinking my decision to walk back alone. Every noise makes me jump and I glance about searching for any danger lurking. Shadows move about, but no one approaches. I look over my shoulder, but all I see is the inky black night. My pace quickens until, finally, I get to the tent I share with Zara and Sage.

I sneak in through the entrance and slowly let the flap close behind me trying to be quiet. Inside is dimly lit from a fire that needs stoked. I cross over to it and add another piece of wood. Once it takes the flame, I find my pallet and climb under all the furs spreading the luani one over the top of them all.

My head hits the bundled fur I tried to craft into a pillow. It's ugly, but it does what it's supposed to.

"Didn't think you were going to be home tonight," Zara says softly from her spot closest to mine.

I jump and suck in a breath. "You scared the crap out of me."

She doesn't apologize. "I was worried about you."

"Why? You knew I was with Benham. I'm a grown woman, you know?"

When Zara remains quiet, the guilt creeps in. I didn't mean to snap at her.

"I used to have an older sister," she says before I can tell her I'm sorry. "You remind me a lot of her, actually."

A sister? She's never said anything before about having a sister. Just shitty parents. My heart hurts at the tone of her voice. It's filled with so much sadness.

"Her name was Amelia. My parents thought it was cute to have daughters with names that started with the first and last letters of the alphabet. She was nine years older and more of a mother to me than my actual one. I used to follow her everywhere when I was little. Not once did she ever make me feel like I was bothering her. She always had time for me and gave the best hugs I'd ever had. The *only* hugs I ever had. I loved her more than anyone on Earth."

Is this why Zara gets so twitchy when we give them to her?

"When I was ten, she came home one day a completely different person. She would spend days locked in her room. If she did come out, she always kept her head down and barely talked to anyone. Not even me." Her voice cracks slightly and she pauses. "Slowly she got better. Never really back to her old self, but she at least talked to me. Asked me how my day was. What I learned in school. Had I made any new friends. Until about six months later, when she just disappeared without a word. Not even a note. One minute she was there, the next minute...*poof.* She was gone."

This time, there's no mistaking the fact she's crying.

She sniffles and in the pale firelight I can see her wiping her face. "Every day I worried about her. Wondered if she was doing okay. Or if she was gone because of something I did or didn't do. I know you're a grown woman, but Amelia was too when she disappeared. So, yeah, I'm going to worry. Even if you're with Benham. I don't want to lose another sister."

Zara's going to have to suck it up, because I scramble over to her pallet and hug her. Which isn't easy with her lying down, but I do my best. "You're not going to lose me."

When she shifts, I just hug her tighter. And then her one free arm drapes across my back and she squeezes me back. We stay like that for several seconds. I can sense Zara's reached her limit so I loosen my hold and sit back on my heels. She stares up at the roof and looks like she's miles away.

"Did you ever find her? Amelia?" I ask quietly.

"Some kids from the bottom tier found her body along the shoreline of the river and called the guards. Because my parents were rich and influential, they actually performed an investigation. According to security video footage, they discovered she jumped from the bridge." Zara huffs out a soft breath. "I don't think they would have even told me. I overheard them talking. To this day, I still don't know why she did it, although I have my suspicions."

God, I can't imagine what she's gone through to lose her sister so horribly. "I know it doesn't help any, but I'm so sorry."

She turns her head toward me and the firelight makes the tears in her eyes sparkle. "Thanks, Mae."

"I'm sorry I was gone for so long and made you worry."

Zara reaches out and grips my hand. "He hasn't made you do anything you don't want to do, has he?"

"No. I'm finally realizing that he wouldn't. Benham hasn't once touched or kissed me without getting my consent first." Except waking up with his hand palming my entire breast. But that doesn't count.

A slow smile creeps up from her. "Kissing, huh? Has he discovered all the really good places to kiss you, yet? What about the naughty, wicked tail?"

My entire face heats. "We've only kissed on the lips and the closest his tail has gotten to me is when he looped my waist with it. Although…"

She jackknifes up when I let the silence hang. "Oh my god, Mae, you can't just stop there. Although what? I want all the details."

"Since I'm not going to stay sleeping with you guys talking, I want all the details, too," Sage grumbles and slowly pushes herself upright while wiping one of her eyes.

Zara and I look at each other and wince. "Sorry, Sage."

Sage waves a hand. "It's fine. Now, what's this?"

I've never had girlfriends to share this kind of stuff with. Of course, my only sexual partner had been David and I never wanted to tell anyone about that. So many regrets fill me. I wish I could have come to Benham a virgin.

"We don't mean to be so pushy," Zara says. "You don't have to tell us if you don't want to."

I rattle my head. "No, that's not it. I was just thinking that I've never talked about…you know, with anyone before. It might just take some getting used to."

"You only have to tell us what you're comfortable with," Sage adds. "It's okay to keep things private."

Zara nods in agreement. "Yep."

It'll be good to tell them. Maybe it will help me get out of my own head. "Okay, we did a little more than kissing. I wanted to make sure I could, you know…do more. So, I put Benham's hand on my boob. First over my shirt. Then under. It felt good, and I didn't freak out or anything."

"Go Maeve," Zara cheers, making me snort.

"After that, we laid down together, just to kiss and touch a little, and I got the courage to take my shirt off. It was a lot, so he just held me. We both fell asleep, and I woke up to him spooning me and his hand on my breast again, except I didn't know it was his at first. For just a second, I panicked a little until Benham stopped touching me and said my name. That's when I realized it was him." I flop my hands. "So, there."

"Should we assume this means you accepted the mate bond?" Sage asks.

I pause for a second and consider it. Slowly, I nod. "Yeah, I think it does. God, this is terrifying, but not like in a bad way. Benham has been so patient with me. He's letting me set the pace which makes me feel like I'm in control. That helps a lot."

"I'm so happy for you, Mae." Zara squeezes my hand.

"Me too," Sage echoes. "I know London and Remi will be as well."

I glance between the two of them. "Thank you guys for being my friends. My sisters. I really do love you."

"We love *you*," Zara tells me and I know she truly means it.

Sage shifts. "Now that we got all the juicy details and declared our undying sisterly love, can I please go back to sleep now?"

"Yes, we're all going to sleep now." I crawl back over to my sleeping pallet while Sage and Zara both lie back down.

I make myself comfortable and bring Benham's luani fur up to my nose and breathe in the woodsmoke and cocoa that has permeated into the hide. I'm pretty sure I fall asleep with a smile on my face.

CHAPTER 17

Benham

Never have I woken to a more glorious morning than this one. Last night with Maeve had been more than I could have dreamed. Deeka has surely blessed me with the bravest and most incredible mate. Every kiss and touch I received were worth the wait and the patience. A male could not ask for a better *keeshla* than my Maeve.

The scent of her still lingers on the furs where she laid. It is a soft, clean smell with a hint of the herbs and roots she harvests with Alanda. I will never take for granted the trust she gifted me by lying in my arms without her chest covering. After her confession, I finally understand the 'bad shit' my mate has gone through. How any male could hurt her is beyond my understanding. No matter how vengeful it might be, I say a prayer to Deeka that the male back on Earth get what is coming to him and that he is punished in some way.

I rise from my furs, wipe myself with the chilled water in the basin on the table, and put on a clean pair of leg coverings. When I return from our hunt, I need to head to the river to wash the ones I have worn the last few days. The ones I wore during the hunt with Talek and Samik were beyond repair.

If we are hunting a luani, then I will need my swords and a spear. The creature used to be plentiful, but over the many seasons their numbers have dwindled. The Krijese would butcher them for nothing more than sport and leave their remains for the shkaba to scavenge. It is no wonder their people were starving. It has been since my fifteenth warm season that I have encountered one. I have spent more time training the young warriors for battle than I have hunted.

Once I have my weapon belt around my waist with a sheathed sword and two daggers attached, a sword in a scabbard slung across my back, and my spear in hand, I head for the central fire. I slept a bit later than I normally do, so Evren, Jodah, and Katem are already almost through with their bowls of kokkra.

"Greetings Benham," Jodah greets me. He's one of the few rare warriors who isn't hesitant with or intimidated by me.

I nod and fill my own bowl before joining the hunters.

"We were planning on heading toward the valley where the ujera lies. It is where the last signs of the luani were seen," Evren says.

The valley is more than seven turns of the sun away from here. Just beyond that is where the Njeri live. Djentar and their leader made some type of trade agreement many seasons ago, while I was still a young warrior. Just before I killed the luani. Except since then, none of their tribespeople have approached us for trading. Perhaps it is the long journey between our villages that prevent it.

I quickly finish my meal, and then I am ready. Turning to the young warriors, I gesture. "Lead the way."

The four of us leave through the front gates of the village where Rojtar stands guard and make our way across the vast length of the bari field in the direction of the valley. The second moon still lingers in the sky and the sun has yet to crest the horizon. Any number of enemies could be hiding within the shadows of the forest that borders the field. The image of the lone male I spotted within the base of the hills only a few turns of the sun ago returns to me. We should be prepared to encounter anything.

I glance at the three young hunters. They speak softly amongst themselves, but it is obvious they are still focused on their surroundings. I shift my grip on my spear and scan the horizon in front of me.

Jodah moves away from the other two and matches pace with me. "How does it feel being mated to a human?"

I glance over at him. The envy is back in his eyes. Of the three of them, he is the oldest but still eight cold seasons younger than me. While he has never specifically mentioned wanting a mate, I have noticed the way his eyes track the unmated females.

"It is both wonderful and terrifying," I admit.

His brow ridges raise. "Terrifying?"

"Human females do not feel the bond like Tavikhi do. There is no guarantee that they will choose to be your mate, no matter what your mating marks say."

"Has your mate chosen you?" he asks. "She has appeared fearful of us."

I will wait to hear it from her lips that she chooses me. I will not assume, but rather must give her the choice.

"I believe she has, but I will not push her if she hasn't. The humans come from a place that does not always treat them well. Many of them have scars, hidden beneath the surface we cannot see."

Jodah is quiet a moment. We travel farther away from the village before he speaks again. "What if the goddess does not deem me worthy of a mate?"

"Why would you think that to be? Perhaps she is still one of the humans that remains in the settlement? Or still on Earth waiting for the next ship to bring her here?" I clap him on the shoulder. "You must not lose faith that Deeka has someone special for you."

I do not want to give Jodah false hope, but I also do not want him to give up hope completely. He nods, but I am not sure I have done a good job convincing him that his fated mate just hasn't found him yet. He falls back and rejoins Evren and Katem, but I can sense his discontent. I send up an extra prayer to Deeka that she will grant Jodah, and any other warrior who wishes for one, his mate.

We do not go much farther when I spot it. I pause my steps and raise my arm over my head to signal I have found something. Luani scat is buried within broken pieces of bari. I scan the field for any other disturbances that might offer a direction the creature might have gone. There are several places where the bari has been bent, but it does not appear to have been made by a four-legged beast.

"Stay alert." I glance back at the three hunters. "Someone else has passed through here within the last turn of the sun. I do not recognize the tracks."

They nod and rest their hands on the hilt of their weapons. I tighten my grip on my spear and motion them forward and to spread out. More luani droppings dot the field and appear to be heading into the forest. I follow them and enter the dense collection of trees. During our trek the sun has appeared brightly in the sky, but the towering trees with branches full of leaves block most of it.

The air grows colder without the heat of the sunshine, and dark shadows blanket the ground. We silently step through the dirt and brush, taking care not to alert anyone or anything that might be nearby of our presence. The air is thick with tension. There are the sounds of the small forest-dwelling animals scurrying and the faint calls of several mellenje in the distance.

Up ahead, a branch cracks. I throw up an arm and we all freeze to listen. There's a flash of color in the distance, but it's gone so quickly I cannot confirm it is the beast we seek. Jodah, Evren, Katem, and I remain rooted to the spot for several more beats of my heart, but all is quiet.

We take only a few steps when a vicious roar echoes in the air and mellenje shoot out of the trees and into the sky. I tighten my grip on my spear and the others draw their swords just as a massive luani comes rushing toward us. This one is nothing like the starving, half-dead one I put out of its misery all those seasons ago. This beast has eaten well and it wants to add us to its food supply.

I leap up into the nearest tree right before it reaches me and drop onto the thing's back while stabbing it in the neck. It bellows and rears up. I lose my hold on my spear as I tumble to the ground. I roll out of striking distance and unsheathe one of my swords. With the small distraction I managed, Jodah and Evren attack from each side, while Katem attacks from the back. It can not strike at all of us at once. It chooses Evren, who barely escapes a swipe from the luani's vicious claws.

Jodah gets in a strike on its foreleg and the creature stumbles, but quickly recovers. Katem slices a rear leg. Once again, the four of us lead a coordinated attack from all sides. This time, when the luani lashes out, its claws rake across Jodah's chest. He cries out, spins, and collapses short distance. Now that the beast has drawn blood, it fights even more viciously.

Evren and Katem circle the injured luani while I take to the trees again. They draw it closer to where I am and as it passes beneath me, I jump and drive my sword straight into the back of its neck. My legs and tail tighten around it and I hold fast to my sword as it attempts to dump me off it again. When it is unsuccessful, I feel its muscles tense beneath me right before it rolls. I barely clear getting pinned beneath its great weight.

However, Evren and Katem attack before it can rise to its feet, and I draw my second sword and join. At last, Evren pierces his blade through its heart and the beast lies still. The sound of our ragged breathing echoes around us. From where he fell, Jodah groans.

"Find some sherim plants and bring me their gethet leaves," I order Katem and rush to the wounded warrior's side.

Katem disappears and Evren helps me gently roll Jodah onto his back. Four bloody gashes line his chest. Evren grabs the water skin from his belt and passes it to me. I uncap it and pour some of the water over the wound to rinse the blood away and get a better look.

Jodah's face is lined with pain and his eyes remain closed. His chest rises and falls with the effort it takes him to breathe. Even with the gethet leaves, I am not sure he will make it. I turn to Evren.

"Gather branches to make a sled."

He nods and gets to work. With my sword, I cut off the bottom of one side of Jodah's leg coverings and use the soft hide to clean the wound as carefully as I can of the dirt that still clings to it. I need to save some of the water to make a paste with the gethet leaves and create a poultice. There are healing properties in the plant, but even the slash across my face isn't nearly as bad as the ones on Jodah's chest. They are deep and continue to bleed.

I should help Evren construct the sled, but if the warrior lying here is to die, I do not want him to be alone when it happens. Instead, I break off a small branch from a nearby tree and manage to carve a crudely shaped vessel with my blade. As I finish, rustling leaves sound behind me and I pivot on my knee with my sword gripped tightly, but it is only Katem returning.

He passes me the leaves and I break them up into small pieces. I dump both them and a bit of water into the vessel and with the hilt of my dagger, grind it up to form a paste. Carefully, I cover the wounds with it. After that, all I can do is pray to Deeka. Soon, Evren returns with long, thick branches and several lengths of vines that grow along the ground within the forest. We construct the sled, using the vines to tie the branches together and then Evren and I lift Jodah and place him on the sled.

"I'll take him." I gesture to our fallen friend. "You two bring the luani."

With that, the three of us begin our long trek back to the village.

CHAPTER 18

Maeve

I've been pacing for at least an hour.

"Oh my god, you're giving me whiplash. Please sit down for five minutes." Zara begs. "Just five minutes."

With a huff, I plop down on my pallet and wrap my luani fur tightly around me to breathe in the wood and cocoa scent that reminds me of Benham. Which only ramps up my anxiety, because what if this luani is the one that gets him? Those things are humungous and dangerous. What if he gets hurt?

"Benham's going to be fine."

I glance at Zara. "You don't know that. The animal they're hunting is vicious. And they've been gone forever."

She cocks her head and purses her lips. "They haven't been gone any longer than normal hunts. Besides, you need to trust your husband and his ability to take care of himself. Benham's a bad ass fighter. It doesn't matter how vicious their prey is, your man could bring it down with only one of his grouchy glares. The luani is the one that should be terrified."

I snort. "I know, you're right. I've just never had someone to worry about like I do with Benham and it's kind of freaking me out. I mean, what if he dies before I tell him I want to be his mate?"

"He's not going to die," Zara says firmly. "Sheesh."

Cries from outside bring my head up. I jump to my feet, nearly losing the hold I have on the fur, and burst out of the tent. Zara is right behind me. I suck in a sharp breath when I finally lay eyes on Benham several tents away in front of the healer's. He's covered in dirt and the hair that usually hangs long and silky down his back is a ratty mess with leaves stuck in it. My gaze drops to the makeshift stretcher he pulls behind him, and the pale body that lies on it.

Zara and I rush toward them as Kyler steps out. We come to an abrupt halt a short distance away. The healer gestures at one of the tribesmen and between the three of them, they manage to lift the injured warrior and carry him inside. I hope he's okay. I've never seen a Tavikhi lose that much color. He's almost not even purple anymore.

For far too long a stretch of time, we stand there waiting for Benham to come out.

"What's going on?" London stops next to us. "I heard one of the warriors is wounded, but no one told me who."

"It was hard to tell," Zara says.

"I'm pretty sure it was Jodah," I add. "Benham told me last night he was going with him and Evren to hunt a luani they'd found signs of."

All I can picture is the scar on my mate's face, given to him by the same animal. Poor Jodah. But then I remember what Benham said about bearing his scars proudly. If the warrior makes it, I hope he feels the same way about them. That they demonstrate his strength in surviving.

Footsteps approach and I glance behind us. Zander's tail brushes London's waist for a brief second before he strides past us and enters the healer's tent. I'm not surprised he's here. Minutes after he goes inside, Benham steps out. His eyes land on me and there's a spark in them. I rush over and lay my hands on his chest.

"Are you okay?"

He gently cradles the side of my face and his tail wraps loosely around my waist. "I am well, *keeshla.*"

I blink. This might be the first time he's called me that. The endearment settles over me like a warm blanket. I reach for his hand. "We should get you cleaned up."

He glances over his shoulder like he's not sure he should leave his friend.

"I'll check on him and let you know if anything changes," Zara offers.

I send her a grateful smile and finally Benham nods. "My thanks."

He lets me lead him to his tent. I grab the torch from outside and bring it inside with us where the fire burns low. My hold loosens on Benham's hand, and I plant the torch in the ground and add another piece of wood to the fire.

"Sit." I point at the chair next to the fire pit.

He takes a seat and I can feel his eyes on me as I grab the cloth from the table and drop it into the basin of water. Careful not to drop it, I bring it over to where he sits and set it on the ground next to him. Thankful that he's at my level, I pluck the dried leaves out of his hair.

"I assume you found the luani?" Or maybe it found them. Only a giant alien lion could cause that much damage.

"We did." Benham's voice is low.

I toss each leaf into the fire and the sweet pungent scent grows stronger making the urge to sneeze great. I sniff a few times to hold it back. Once I've inspected his hair and confirmed there's nothing left, I try to finger comb through the knots.

"There is a hair implement in the chest."

I meet his gaze and he gestures to the other side of the tent. Glad for that at least, I open the lid and have to rifle through a few pairs of pants, but I find it. Careful not to tug too hard, I slowly draw the comb through the length of Benham's hair. He's going to have to wash it in the river to get it fully clean, but at least it's something. Once I'm finished, I set the comb on the table and wring out the water in the cloth before washing away the dirt that clings to his skin.

"Did you kill it?" I run the cloth across his shoulder and down his arm.

"We did," he repeats.

I shouldn't be glad the animal is dead, but I know that its meat means the tribespeople will have more food to survive the cold season. Plus, the fur will provide someone some much needed warmth.

I rinse out the cloth and make my way to Benham's other side. My gaze follows the path my hand takes over the dips and swells of his muscles. A flicker of heat, low in my belly spreads out from my center to the rest of my body and grows in its intensity.

Again I rinse out the dirty cloth and with a deep breath, I nudge his legs apart and step into the vee of them. Benham jerks his head up, but I keep my eyes on his chest where I wash next. His ginormous, but gentle, hand lightly covers mine. Water trails down his stomach and soaks into the waistband of his leather pants.

"Maeve?"

I blink and finally meet his gaze. My cheeks are warm, but my body is warmer. Not from the fire burning near us either. It's him. My husband—my mate.

"Let me. Please."

Benham's eyes burn into mine, until he slowly lowers his hand to his knee. I move in closer and swipe the cloth over his chest and down his ribbed abs. All without taking my eyes off his. I've given up all pretense that I'm actually cleaning him anymore when I drop to cloth to the ground where it may or may not land in the basin.

I thread my fingers through his hair and lean in to press my lips to Benham's. He parts them, and my tongue swoops in to glide across his. My fur slides off my shoulders to hit the ground as well, but I'm so hot right now I don't even need it. It's as though my blood is on fire heating me from the inside. The kiss deepens and I move close enough that my breasts press against him. It barely eases the ache in them. Only Benham's touch will take it away completely.

A heavy weight wraps around my waist and grips my hips. I wait for the trapped sensation to swarm over me, but it doesn't. Only more heat and a throbbing right where I need him the most. My clit pulses as blood flows to it. It matches the thumping beat of my heart.

I pull my head back, only enough to murmur against Benham's lips. "Touch me."

"Is this truly what you want?"

I nip Benham's bottom lip in response and rub my needy breasts against him. It's like I've lit a fuse on a stick of dynamite. Now I just wait for the explosion. I already know it's going to be an epic one. His hand leaves my hip and spears through my hair. He clasps the back of my head and tilts it the way he wants to deepen this kiss. It's like he wants to consume me. I'm ready to let him.

When a warm hand brushes across my bare belly, I jump. Not from fear. Benham tries to take it away, and I grab him to hold him in place.

"Touch me," I repeat in a stronger, more confident tone.

Thank Deeka, or whoever else might be up there, because he does. He slides his hand under my shirt and engulfs my breast in his hand kneading it gently. Molding it. My nipple hardens, and he plucks the sensitive tip. A shudder runs through me, and I press myself further into his touch.

As though Benham's done this a thousand times, his mouth leaves mine and runs along my jaw and my neck where he laves his tongue in the crease where it meets my shoulder. He breathes in deeply, and his rough growl vibrates through my entire body. I'm bombarded with sensations I've never experienced before. So much plea-sure I didn't know existed. Is it always like this? If so, I don't ever want it to end.

"May I taste you, Maeve?" Benham rumbles into my ear.

That could mean so many things, and I'm pretty sure he's not talking about my lips. I take a small step back, enough that I'm still close enough to touch him. My fingers dance along the crest of his shoulders. If he can face down the same beast who scarred him so long ago and come out victorious, then I can show the same courage. I reach for the hem of my shirt and pull it up and over my head, tossing it off to the side somewhere.

Benham's gaze lands on my chest and his vertical, cat-like pupils dilate. Despite the warmth inside the tent and flowing through me, my nipples peak under the intensity of his stare. He palms both breasts again, his hand so large he covers them entirely. I lean into his touch. Based on his apparent fascination with them, I'm going to take my husband as a tit man. He hasn't paid nearly enough attention to my butt for me to think he's an ass man. I giggle at that.

"What does my mate find so humorous?"

I lift my gaze to his and his lips are tilted up in amusement. My cheeks grow hot. If I can trust Benham with my body, I can trust him with my words. "Back on Earth, there's this long-time…joke, I guess you could say, that a guy is either a tit man or an ass man. Meaning they either love a woman's breasts the most or her butt—ass—the most. I was just thinking that you're probably a tit man considering how much you like to touch mine."

Benham is silent for a beat and then he laughs. Oh my god, it totally transforms his face. If I thought he was gorgeous before, it's nothing compared to this. He's absolutely stunning. This is the first time I've ever seen him laugh. I want to do whatever I can to see it happen again.

His laughter slows to a chuckle. "I do believe I might be a what you call tit male. Although I will admit I have not given enough attention to your ass to know if I love it less."

Even though I can tell he's trying to be funny, the thought of Benham staring at my ass sends a ping through me and makes me want to find out. "Maybe we should perform an experiment."

I slowly turn and take a step forward. Despite the heat burning my cheeks, I glance over my shoulder. Sure enough, his gaze is focused on my butt. I've always secretly thought I had a great ass. He reaches out and grips my hips. His hands are so large, he easily spans them. When he rubs his thumbs up and down my butt cheeks, I squirm with need. It doesn't matter that I'm still wearing pants. It's like Benham's touch sears away any barrier between us.

He lifts his head and one side of his mouth kicks up. "It is a very fine ass, but I still think these are my favorite. I am most definitely a tit male."

Making his point, he slides his hands up my sides and cups both breasts from behind. My laugh is cut off midway and I stumble back against his chest. While holding firmly onto me, he kisses his way up my shoulder and once again in the crook of my neck. I tilt my head to give him better access and lay my hands over his urging him to squeeze me a bit harder.

Arousal spikes through me.

As much as I want to continue feeling his hands on me, I want to give him something since he's given so much to me. I slowly turn back around to face him and palm his cheeks.

"I want you to taste me, now. Please."

His pupils dilate again and his gaze drops to my chest. Far too slowly, Benham lowers his head and his thick tongue darts out to lap at my nipple. With that single caress, I'm completely done for.

CHAPTER 19

BENHAM

Maeve's flavor is like nothing that has ever touched my tongue before. It is as addictive as the shurup nectar the humans favor in their kokkra. She is sweet but with a hint of spice. Does she taste this good everywhere? I want to find out. If not this night, then maybe another. I draw her whole chest mound—breast—into my mouth and taste the sweetness of her.

My mate's blunt claws dig into my shoulders as she leans more into me. Small noises spill from her lips and I lift my gaze to hers without letting her go. Pleasure spreads across her face and she is focused on where we are connected. The color of her eyes has darkened.

This is what my baba and nene had and what I did not know I needed or think I wanted. A closeness like no other with a mate. Without Deeka I never would have had this and I send up a prayer of thanks and a hope that I can please my *keeshla*. I give the same attention to her other breast and it tastes just as wonderful as the other. Before I have had my fill, Maeve pulls back. Afraid I have done something wrong, I open my mouth to apologize, but she speaks first.

"I want to lay down together in the furs."

There is no hesitation in her request. I unwind my tail that has found its way around her waist and stand. Somehow my mate appears even smaller in this moment with her dark-stained cheeks and shy glances at my painfully erect cock behind my leg coverings. Maeve takes my hand and leads me over to my furs. Together we lower ourselves. My *keeshla* lies on her side facing me and I wait patiently for her to lead us wherever it is she is ready to go.

Unable to resisting touching her in some way, though, I reach out and caress her cheek, brushing the two-colored hair off it. I am anxious to see her with only the pale hair she loves so much.

"Have I told you how beautiful you are?"

Maeve ducks her head and shakes it gently before lifting it up again. "No," she whispers.

"Your beauty outshines all the dreams and wishes inside my head. Not just here,"—I brush my finger down her face and chest until I reach her heart—"but also here."

Water pools in her eyes and a droplet spills out the side leaving a wet track. "The whole time you were gone today, I was so worried something would happen to you and I wouldn't get a chance to tell you…I want to be your mate."

I have never heard sweeter words than those. "My brave *keeshla*. Thank you for the honor you have given me. I will do all I can to prove you will not regret it."

Maeve nods. "I trust you. Will you make love to me?"

A kiss is my answer. My lips claim hers and she opens for my tongue to sweep inside. I pay close attention to the sounds my mate makes and what she likes best. Every touch is for her pleasure. I want to destroy all her bad memories and replace them with ones that remind her how it feels to be loved by a male who cares for her and will never hurt her. Maeve will teach me how she wants to be touched in every way.

I break the kiss and rest my brow ridges gently against her softness. "Show me what you like and how to please you."

She breathes in deeply and takes my hand in hers. I let her guide it downward until it reaches her waist. "Touch me. Down there."

Taking my time in case I have misunderstood, I slide my hand along the edge of her leg coverings and dip beneath them. When she does not stop me, I continue gliding my fingers downward until I encounter a small tuft of hair. My eyes widen at the dampness within it. I move my finger again and, when I encounter a hard nub, Maeve sucks in a breath. She makes a tiny shift closer.

"You have a nipple down here as well?"

My mate laughs. "That is my clit."

"Clit? What does it do?"

She raises a shoulder. "It's just for pleasure. To help a woman orgasm."

I explore this pleasure center with my finger and watch Maeve's face intently. After much testing, I soon discover the amount of pressure and speed which makes her gasp and squirm in my arms. Her chest rises and falls quickly and little moans come from her mouth. They are the most perfect sounds. I do not stop, because I want my mate to reach her peak.

With each beautiful noise she makes, and every time she jerks her hips, pushing herself against my finger, my cock hardens even more. All male Tavikhi have mating nodes that open and secrete a fluid meant to give our mates greater pleasure. I can feel my mating fluid leaking from them, preparing for my *keeshla*.

"I want to see your release." I find the rhythm Maeve loves best against her swollen clit and don't stop until her whole body tenses and she shakes.

She cries out and grinds herself against my hand, shuddering until at last she sags with a heavy exhale. Her eyes flutter open, and a drowsy but satisfied smile lights up her face. "That was amazing."

Pride wells up inside. "I am glad to offer you pleasure."

My mate's cheeks darken to the color of the manerrat berry. "We're not done, I hope."

"Not if you do not wish to be."

Maeve traces the mating marks on my sides. "I do not wish to be."

Then I am happy to give her whatever she desires. I bring my hand out from where I left it inside her leg coverings. "May I take these off?"

She nods. Rising up on my knees I gently nudge her so she lies on her back. Her eyes remain on me as I tug at the cloth guarding her from me. She lifts her hips and I slide her leg coverings down until they are completely off. I toss them on top of her chest covering and stare down at her. Her breasts rise toward the sky and her waist dips before flaring out to form her lovely hips.

Between her legs is the pale hair that covers her cunt. It is a shade darker than the pale part on her head. The sweet musky scent of her arousal fills our tent. While I would like to bring my nose closer and breathe her in even deeper, my instincts tell me to wait. There will always be another night. But this first time with us together should be slow and easy. We will take our time with pleasuring each other. Discovering what the other likes.

"Am I so different from the female Tavikhi?" Maeve moves as though to cover herself. I gently clasp her hands and draw them away.

"Not so different. Although the females do not have that sensitive nub you have. A clit. At least not to my knowledge. Your body is the only one I have ever touched. The only one I will *ever* touch. It is perfection."

My mate glances away from me, but then meets my gaze again. "I want to see you."

I nod and remove my own leg coverings. Lying back, I let Maeve look all she wants. She sits partway up and her eyes shift to stare at my cock. Her mouth parts and a sudden image of her wrapping her lips around my length makes me groan. She swallows and turns her gaze to me.

"Can I touch you?"

"Of course."

Tentatively, she reaches out, pausing just before her fingers touch me, and then—glorious ecstasy. Maeve traces a path up my length, grazing across the sensitive—and open— nodes that line it. She circles one with her finger and draws mating fluid from the tiny hairs that fill it.

"What are these?" Her tone is hushed. She strokes over it again and a shudder courses through me.

"Those are my mating nodes. They are similar to your clit in that they provide pleasure. The fluid within them will release and stimulate inside you."

Maeve lifts her eyes to meet mine as she brings her finger that glistens with wetness up to her mouth. Her tongue flicks out to taste it and I nearly release my essence right then. She does it again and laps up the rest of it. "Mmm, you taste good."

I groan. Her words are exquisite torture. Made even more so when she wraps as much of her hand around me as she can and glides it up and down my length. I grit my teeth to keep my control that is quickly unraveling. The need to be inside her is all-consuming.

"I want to feel you inside me," Maeve says as though reading my thoughts.

"Lie down and let me bring my *keeshla* pleasure."

She releases me with a slow drag of her fingertips and moves to her back. My mate is so small. I worry I will hurt her in some way. Carefully I settle between her legs and make sure to keep my weight off her. Her big eyes stare up at me.

"Is all well, my Maeve?"

She nods and lays her hands on my sides. "Yes. I need you."

Reaching between us, I guide myself to her cunt and pause. "You will tell me if it hurts in any way?"

"I will. Please."

I find her opening and enter her a fraction at a time. She is still wet from her previous release and I slide through the slickness that eases my way into her. I keep my eyes on her face, always watching for her reactions. Maeve bites her bottom lip and gasps as more of my length enters her. Her blunt claws dig into me and she spreads her legs farther open so I can settle more deeply between them.

At long last, I am fully seated inside her. I grit my teeth with the urge to thrust. Her cunt squeezes me so tightly. So perfectly. My *keeshla* raises her gaze, and water leaks from her eyes. I try to withdraw for fear I have hurt her, but Maeve wraps her legs around me and pulls me more tightly against her.

"No, stay," she nearly begs.

"Why do your eyes leak?"

She sputters a small laugh. "Because I never thought I could feel like this. It's magical. I've spent so long being scared and guarding my heart. But with your kindness and your patience you've managed to heal what I thought had been broken inside me."

"There is nothing about you that is broken, my Maeve. You have the heart of a warrior."

"I'm so glad Deeka brought me here to be your mate. She knew you were exactly what I needed."

I brush my finger over her bottom lip. "And you are everything I need. My soul light shines my love for you."

More water leaks from her eyes. "I've finally realized I love you, too. Now, please make love to me."

Slowly, I move, my thrusts shallow at first and gaining with speed. Our mating fluids slick together, guiding us both closer to our release. I slide my tail between us and find her clit. Soon, Maeve is writhing beneath me and clutching me hard. Her moans and cries are a pleasant note in my ear. I will not last much longer.

Harder and deeper I push in and out, and rub at the swollen bead at the top of her cunt until my mate goes rigid beneath me and she calls out my name. She clenches down on my cock and that is all it takes. Only two more strokes and I spill my seed inside her. The most intense pleasure I have ever known washes over me. Small tremors still pulse through my mate's body. At last, our breaths even out and my Maeve lets out a contented sigh.

I gently withdraw from her tight channel and roll to my side, bringing her with me. She curls against me with so much trust and I wrap my arm around her as she lays her head on my abdomen. Her light touches caress my mating marks that tingle with warmth.

"Thank you for making our first time so beautiful," my *keeshla* says.

"It was the most wondrous thing ever." My gaze lands on the chest containing my nene and baba's things. I glance down at Maeve who looks so peaceful and content. "I'd like to give you something."

She tilts her head back. "Give me something?"

I nod and sit up. She follows, holding a fur to cover her bare body. With great care, I remove items from the chest until I find the soft hide that contains what I seek. I bring it back to our furs and settle in beside my mate. I peel back the hide until I uncover what's inside. Despite the many seasons since she's been gone, it still holds a hint of my nene's scent. I pass it to Maeve, who holds her hands out and gently takes it from me. She sets it on her lap and reaches for the item on top.

When she lifts out the small chest covering, the crystals decorating it sparkle with the reflection of the firelight. She gasps and lifts her gaze to mine. "Oh my god, Benham. This is so beautiful."

My mate sets it down and brings out the matching leg covering. She tenderly strokes the leather and water fills her eyes.

"They belonged to my nene. She wore it at her and my baba's private mating ceremony. When you are ready, I would like for you to wear it at ours."

Maeve carefully sets the coverings next to her, scrambles on her knees over to me, and throws her arms around my waist. "Thank you for the amazing gift. I would be honored to wear it."

I hold her for several beats before letting her go. She returns to her spot in our furs and gently folds the chest and leg coverings and places them back in the protective hide.

"Will you keep it safe again for me until I wear it for you?" she asks.

"Of course." I place it back in the chest and return to Maeve's side.

Once again, I lie down and my mate immediately presses herself against me. My heart is full and my soul light shines brightly. I kiss the top of my *keeshla's* head and she raises up to kiss my lips. She pulls back and stares down at me.

"I love you."

"I love you as well." I draw her close and show her how much.

CHAPTER 20

Maeve

It's incredible how someone's entire life can change in just one week. It's only been seven days since Benham and I sealed our mate bond for the first time, and yet I feel like a completely different person. One who walks a little taller. Smiles a little bigger. And loves a lot more.

Four months ago, I thought I was going to die. But today I have a wonderful, if not simple, life with best friends and a mate who worships and adores me. I have to pinch myself sometimes to make sure I'm not dreaming.

The dull cracking sound of wood against wood grows louder as I head in the direction of the training arena. Benham is working with the children today, helping them with their fighting skills. Change is happening to us all around. My man is attempting to become less of a loner who keeps to himself. He's also working on becoming more patient, mostly with the adult men who have joined the warriors in their daily training and hunting sessions, including a few from the human settlement.

With the threat of the Krijese gone, and with a lot of communication—as well as patience—the Tavikhi and the other humans are interacting more. The ones from the settlement often come to the village and vice versa. Some of the warriors hope to find their mate amongst any of the single women living there.

As for Benham and me, we must be influencing each other, because I'm making an effort to grow my confidence and get rid of the fear that's been haunting me for a year.

"Greetings, Maeve," one of the elders approaching me says.

I smile and wave. "Hi, Alesha. I was going to come by later with that pair of Benham's pants—leg covering—that need repairing, if that's okay?"

She nods. "You are always welcome in our tent."

"Thank you." I wave again. "I'll see you later then."

I pass several more tribespeople who nod or say hello until I come to a stop at the top of the hill and scan the large arena below. Ten children, paired off in five sets of two, spar against each other with small wooden swords and wooden staffs similar to Remi's.

Most are Tavikhi children, but I count four humans. Three boys and—I grin—one girl. The smile slips for a second.

That could have been Lucy. Laughing and playing and getting to grow older. I send a prayer up to Deeka or whatever other divine entity there might be that she's in a better place.

The lone girl, Cecily, is paired off with Talek, whose little tail thrashes behind him as she gives his sword a good crack that makes him stumble. I chuckle at his shocked expression and carefully make my way down the slope holding the fur I'm always wearing and not just because it keeps me warm. I hang it in the tent I now share with Benham every night so it absorbs his scent of smoke and cocoa. That way, I get to have a reminder of him every day while he's either hunting or training. I can breathe in its fragrance whenever I want.

I'm almost to the bottom when his gaze shifts and our eyes meet. The same flutter in my belly starts up and my heart races. His lips curl up sharply and I nearly stop breathing like I do every time Benham smiles like that at me. He's gorgeous and all mine. Finally I reach him and step straight into his arms.

His hold tightens giving me the kind of hug I love so much. "Greetings, *keeshla.*"

I lean back and come up on my tiptoes as high as I can. He meets me the rest of the way for a lingering kiss. "Greetings to you, as well. How goes the training session?"

The soles of my feet touch the ground again, and I stay within Benham's embrace but turn sideways so I can stare out at the children. He barely loosens his hold around my shoulders and the familiar and comforting weight of his tail sits on my waist.

"They are improving daily. Or at least they are when not too busy playing and doing nothing more than chasing each other around the arena," he says with a soft chuckle.

I'm glad he's teaching them to be tough, but also letting them be children. He's going to make a wonderful father someday. Something I'm beginning to hope is sooner rather than later. I would love a little girl with his hair and beautiful eyes. My gaze shifts to Talek again. And let's not forget the adorable tail. London and I have both talked about our desire for kids. Remi isn't in any hurry. She's enjoying the hunting and fighting too much. Another heavy bout of sadness comes out of nowhere and I rest my head on Benham's abdomen.

His palm grazes my cheek. "What troubles you, *keeshla*?"

It amazes me how easily he can read me. Then again, I have almost no difficulty with him, either.

"I'm worried about Sage. She's barely left the healer's tent in days. Zara says she hasn't been back in their tent to sleep, either. The last time I checked on her there were dark circles under her eyes and she looked like she hasn't been eating well, if at all." We all feel helpless. "London and I have brought her several meals, but I'm not sure she's touched them."

Benham strokes my hair. "Deeka will watch over her. Just continue doing what you can. All will work out."

God, I hope so. Zara is taking it hard. She told me it feels like she's losing another sister. But my mate is right. We just need to be here for her and if she's not taking care of herself, then we'll do it for her.

"All right, that is enough for today," he calls out to the children.

They let out a collective sigh, although I can't tell if it's relief or disappointment.

"Eat well and get some rest tonight. Tomorrow we continue training."

This time their groans are obvious, but Benham only chuckles lightly. We stand together as the children clamber up the hill until the last one disappears past the rise. I turn into his arms and tip my head back to stare up at him.

"I've missed you, today." I rub myself against him so there's no mistaking my meaning.

Benham's eyes flare and against my stomach there's a growing hardness. "And I you."

"Maybe we should go back to our tent and you can show me how much." I've never seen myself as a seductress, but with my mate it is a lot easier than I expected. Maybe because he makes me feel sexy and wanted.

Before I can guess his intent, he sweeps me off my feet with one arm behind my back and the other behind my knees. I screech out a laugh.

"Oh my god, what are you doing? Put me down."

"I am taking my mate back to our tent so I may pleasure her for hours before the evening meal," Benham says, not even breaking stride. "Now be still."

Since there's no use fighting him on it, especially since I enjoy being held in his arms, I snuggle closer against his chest and rest my cheek on his shoulder. A devious little voice whispers in my ear though. Listening to it, I lift my head and plant kisses wherever I can reach and flick my tongue out to taste his cocoa-scented skin along his jaw and neck. My life would be even more perfect if he actually tasted like chocolate as well. But I still love the smokey wood flavor I get instead.

Benham nearly stumbles but catches himself. He growls, a low rumble that vibrates through me and lands straight between my thighs. I clench them together and shift.

"My *keeshla* is playing with fire."

I take another lick before meeting his molten eyes. "But only you can make me burn."

Without releasing his gaze, I nip his flesh and he hisses. I soothe the sting with my tongue. Benham's pace picks up until he's at a slow jog and within seconds we're outside our tent. He doesn't even release me. Just shifts his grasp, flings the hide door flap aside, and ducks inside.

As usually someone has already been in and stoked the fire so the interior of our home is toasty warm. It'll only get hotter from here. I can't wait to go up in flames. Already my body is getting ready for him. I'm wet and getting wetter, especially when he lowers me to my feet and I slide down the whole length of his body. I shiver at the raw desire in Benham's gaze.

"I need you." This is the reason I sought him out at the training arena in the first place.

He yanks my shirt up and tosses it away. "I will always give my beautiful mate what she wants."

This time when bends, it's to palm my ass and lift. My legs wrap around his waist on instinct and my naked breasts flatten against his hard chest making my nipples tighten even more. I pant with want. Slowly, Benham lowers us to our furs and the second my back touches them, his scalding mouth closes over my breast.

"Yes," I hiss with pleasure.

I thread my fingers through his hair and clutch him to me. The contrasting hot and cold from one bared breast to the other that's being feasted on makes my body go haywire. So many sensations batter me including the friction he's generating rubbing himself between my thighs. With each movement he catches my clit and I shudder.

"Show me where you want my touch," Benham demands in the tone I've discovered makes me soaking wet.

He's testing my boundaries of pleasure, but never without my consent. But his commands thrill me in a way that I won't—can't—say no. They make me go wild. I push his head farther down my body with a shiver as he rains kisses down my belly to the waistband of my pants. He lifts his gaze and drags them down my legs with his lips following in their path.

I part my thighs farther and Benham's breath is like an inferno across my sensitive clit. He flicks his tongue against the bit of flesh, and I nearly erupt, I'm already strung so tight. A devious smile lights up his face and he buries it where I'm empty and wanting. I cry at as my mate feasts. The wet sounds and his low grumbles make me squirm. When his tongue spears my channel, I buck. It's too much. Too intense.

"Does my *keeshla* like having her cunt tasted?"

Benham's been working on his dirty talk, something I wasn't sure I'd be into. Sometimes I can't decide if I should be embarrassed or if I want even more filth to come out of his mouth. Today, I want more. I nod frantically.

"I want to hear you say it." His teeth graze my clit and I cry out. "Tell me how much you love having me lap up all your sweet juice. That you need my tongue to slide deep inside you, filling you up, but still will not satisfy you completely until my cock takes its place. Tell me you want me to consume every last drop of wetness that spills from your cunt until you shatter, and then fuck you hard until you shatter again."

My head thrashes side to side. "Yes, please. Fuck me."

That's all it takes. Benham latches onto my clit and sucks it hard. At the same time something thick fills me. He thrusts his finger in and out. There's a slight stretch when he adds a second one. Tension builds in me, and I'm wound so tight. My clit pulses and tingles and deep within it the nerves spark. My entire body shakes and twitches as my orgasm hits. Sounds I didn't know I could make spill from my lips.

I'm buzzing with pleasure and open my eyes. Benham's yanking his pants off so fast, I wait for them to rip. He covers me again long before the rippling waves of my release have settled and buries himself to the hilt in a single thrust. I cry out and dig my nails into his back anchoring him to me. He holds himself still, letting me adjust to having his thickness inside me.

"Your cunt grips me so tight. I do not ever want to leave," Benham rasps above me.

I have to tip my head back to meet his eyes because he's so much taller, even lying down. "I don't want you to leave either."

Nobody ever told me sex could be this good. This perfect. Maybe it only happens between two people who love each other. I lock my ankles behind his back and grip his sides to urge him to move. He does, with shallow thrusts at first that lengthen with each roll of his hips until he's pounding hard into me. Benham hits me so deep inside that it almost borders on pain, but I won't tell him to stop. I know the pleasure waiting at the end is worth it, especially when soft brushes against my interior walls spreading his mating fluids around stimulate every nerve ending with pure ecstasy.

Cool air sweeps over the sweat slicking across our bodies, but the heat of his flesh sizzles through me and sets my blood on fire. "Please. More."

My brain can't form complete sentences. It only craves one thing. Release.

Benham's grunts join my mewling sounds as he pushes me closer to my peak. He's braced himself on his elbows above me with my head caged in between them. His pelvis grinds against mine and grazes my clit with each thrust. Something swirls around the fleshy nub and I realize it's his tail. The combined sensation of being so full and the intense pressure on the swollen bead is too much.

My vision fills with a kaleidoscope of colors and I cry out Benham's name. Only a few thrusts later, the tendons in his neck tighten, and he roars. Warm fluid spreads inside me and for a second, I hope that we made a baby. Benham's rasping breaths slow but his chest still heaves until it too moves at its normal pace. Carefully he pulls out of me and rolls off me and onto his side. I lazily—content-edly—move as well until we're face-to-face.

He drags the furs up over us and brushes a few stray strands of hair stuck to my cheek back behind my ear. "I was not too rough?"

I lay my palm on his chest, directly over his heart. "Never. It was perfect."

"*You* are what is perfect," Benham says. "I thank Deeka every day that she brought you to Tavikh. My life was dull before you arrived. Now, it is filled with the most beautiful colors and you are directly at their center. Never has a male been as blessed as me. My soul light shines brightly for you and will until I travel into the lands of the goddess."

My heart swells with all the love I have for Benham. "I didn't think I could love anyone as much as I love you. And if you think Deeka has blessed you, she has done even more so for me. You are the other half of *my* soul and will be until I too travel into her lands."

He wraps me tightly in his embrace and I snuggle closer. I'm the most content I have ever been. Whatever path my life had been on before, I know, deep down in my heart, this is always where I was being led. To this planet. With this male, who healed my broken heart and glued all the pieces of it back together with his love.

EPILOGUE

Sage

For the nearly six months I've been on Tavikh, I've tried to atone for what I did by working with the Tavikhi healer as his apprentice. And for every day of each one of those months, I wait for the next ship to arrive from Earth with the authorities aboard prepared to take me back so I can be punished. Except no one has. Yet.

I strip the platform of the soiled furs that had provided cushioning beneath the last of one of the warriors injured in an attack against the village over a week ago. Kyler, the healer and my boss, cleared the male to return to return to light training, but with strict orders to come see him again if he experienced any pain.

They'll need to be washed after I put fresh ones down. Thankfully, it isn't often that we need the platforms. Most injuries I help treat are minor. A cut here and there when a sword goes rogue in its wielder's hand and they manage to make contact with another warrior during a training session. They cap the ends for safety, but they've been known to fall off. So, I've learned how to stitch a wound, treat a fever, a headache, and make a poultice.

The worst thing I've seen is someone's insides. And stab wounds. Several that have gone in the front and out the back. The male that just left a few hours ago, nearly died from infection. Kyler was here most of the time, but I managed to offer my services for several hours so he could get some rest, with the promise to come get him if need be.

I place clean furs out and toss the bundled up soiled ones in a basket in the corner. Once I've taken inventory of what medicines and supplies we're running low on, I'll walk down to the river and launder them. The cold season is here which means the river is freezing. It's been a pain in the ass, but the girls and I have had to create a fire pit in the bathing area and heat the water we use to bathe. We can't tolerate getting in the water anymore. Which means we're really only able to clean the important bits. I haven't washed my hair in three days.

What I wouldn't give for a nice, long, hot shower. Hell, I'd take a bathtub. I know the Tavikhi have them. Or at least what passes for one. Zander, the leader of the tribe, brought one into his tent after he mated my friend London. If I had any money, I'd pay her to let me use it. Just once. Of course, that also means I'd have to fill and empty it. It might almost be worth it, though.

I carefully catalog every thing and make a mental note of what Kyler is out of or low on. Later I'll ask one of the warriors to go with me into the nearby forest so I can pick some of the herbs and plants that we use to make tinctures and salves. I grab the basket and toss a few of the green berries everyone uses as a soap on top. Bracing myself for the cold, I step outside and head for the river.

It's not a long trek, but crap it's chilly. At least the sun is shining bright so it takes a bit of the cold nip out of the air. I'm curious what the true winter is going to bring when the snow hits the ground. How us humans are even going to manage is beyond me. According to Talek, it can get as high as his waist, which puts it at right about knee level for London and me. Between the six of us, we're average height. Remi and Eloise are taller while Zara and Maeve are a couple inches shorter than me.

I glance around and observe my surroundings. Ever since Remi spotted a lone Krijese just on the other side of the river a couple weeks ago, we've all been a little twitchy. But also more cautious. I reach the water and kneel down next to it, getting as close as I can without falling in. Small amounts of blood get washed downriver and before long, I've cleaned all the furs as best I can. I wring out the water and hang them over the edge of the basket and head back to the healer's tent.

Kyler's inside when I step through the entrance.

"Greetings, Sage. I wondered if you were at the river."

I raise my arms slightly to lift the basket. "Figured I should get these cleaned and drying in front of the fire since all your patients have been discharged."

"They are your patients as well," he reminds me whenever I exclude myself from this job.

It just doesn't feel right calling them mine, when I barely know what I'm doing half the time and Kyler's the true healer. Plus, guilt keeps me from taking any credit. I set down the basket and grab the handmade drying rack to set up near the fire. After I've got it assembled and in place, I hang each fur over the bars, keeping as much distance between them to give the heat a chance to reach every part.

Loud cries comes from just outside. Kyler and I exchange a glance and he walks out. I can hear him yelling at someone for help and then a few seconds later, the door flap opens and he, along with Benham and another warrior, are carrying an injured Tavikhi inside.

"Oh, god." He looks dead. He's so pale to almost not even be lavender anymore. Black blood covers his chest. Some dried. Some not. A poultice is packed within a massive area, but doing nothing to hide the four jagged slashes that run from one arm pit nearly down to the opposite hip.

"Lay him on the platform," Kyler commands the two warriors.

It wakes me from whatever trance I'm in. I rush to pour some ground up burim root in a small cup and mix it with water. How he's still alive has to be a miracle. Behind me, I can hear Kyler gathering what he's going to need to suture his wounds. What kind of animal did this to him? I hurry back over and gently slide my hand under his head so I can raise it and try to get some of the pain reliever down his throat. This close I recognize him.

"Jodah, I need you to drink this for me, okay?" I stare down at his face and place the cup at his lips.

I'm careful to slowly pour the water in so he doesn't choke, only giving him a small amount at a time. Most of it drips out of the corners of his mouth, but I have to hope that at least some of it is making its way down his throat.

"By the goddess," Kyler rasps out in a harsh whisper.

From somewhere on the other side of the tent is an audible exclamation. I jerk my gaze toward the healer, but his wide eyes are focused on Jodah. Is he dead? I glance down to check that he's still breathing and freeze. Not because of the warrior's wounds, but because of the bright and darkening tattoos—mating marks—that appear on Jodah's ribcage. They're perfectly formed on his uninjured side, but the marks are broken and deformed on the side where the claw marks have sliced through his skin. The swirled lines and designs grow darker on both arms as well.

Kyler lifts his eyes to meet mine. "Another mating."

At first what I'm seeing and hearing doesn't process, but slowly my brain kicks in. After all these months on Tavikh, the goddess the Tavikhi worship has decided that Jodah and I are supposed to be fated mates. Just when he could —probably will—die. Maybe I don't need to worry about the authorities arriving on Tavikh to drag me back to Earth to face my punishment. Because *this* is my punishment. Giving me a mate, only for him to be taken away from me.

Maybe it's also Deeka that brought me to this village so I could become someone who tries to save lives in order to make up for the one I took.

Thank you so much for reading! Please consider leaving a review.

For Sage and Jodah's story, check out Fated to the Alien Rebel

---

Sage

I've built a new life on the planet Tavikh, spending every day seeking penance. And despite witnessing three of my new-found friends find their fated mate, I don't dare hope to find mine. Not when there's a chance someone from Earth will arrive to take me back to face the consequences for what I did.

But when a gravely wounded warrior is brought into the healer's tent, a single touch from me triggers his mating marks to appear. Maybe my punishment isn't having to return to my planet, but rather being given a mate only for him to be taken from me.

Jodah

Ever since Deeka blessed the other warriors with their fated mates, I have wondered if the goddess will find me equally worthy. After awakening from a grievous injury, I discover it is the healer's apprentice she has chosen for me. Except, despite my mating marks, I do not feel the mate bond within, leaving me to question whether Deeka made a mistake in her choice. Or perhaps I am being tested.

As I recover, and we spend more time together, there is something about my mate that makes me hope the bond may still form. Now I have to decide if I will follow where my heart is leading me or reject the female who may or may not be mine.

Warriors of Tavikh

Fated to the Alien Warrior
Fated to the Alien Hunter
Fated to the Alien Grump
Fated to the Alien Rebel

About the Author

Erin Hale resides in the South where the summer humidity sucks the breath right out of you. She's mom to the best dog on the planet. In her free time, she enjoys reading about swoon-worthy aliens (and secretly wishes one would land on Earth) and monsters alike. She also loves traveling the globe and can be seen most often in any of the pubs in the UK—where the weather is much more acceptable—with a raspberry gin and lemonade in hand.

www.ingramcontent.com/pod-product-compliance
Lightning Source LLC
Chambersburg PA
CBHW061530310726

48972CB00008B/2401